A Girl on the Plane

A Ryeland Press Book

By

Maggie McIntyre

DEDICATION

This book is dedicated to my friends working in international development, who continue to campaign tirelessly on behalf of young girls and boys whose lives are blighted by being trafficked across the world.

DISCLAIMER

This work is fiction, and is purely the work of the author's imagination. Any similarity to people or organizations in real life is purely coincidental, and no reference to any events, past or present is intended.

ALSO WRITTEN BY MAGGIE MCINTYRE
AND AVAILABLE FROM
RYELAND PRESS:

ISABEL'S HEALING (ISBN 9798650898733)
HEATWAVE (ISBN 9798677313929)
WILDFIRE (ISBN 9798550424988)

A Girl on the Plane

Published in 2020 by Ryeland Press

Copyright © Maggie McIntyre

First Edition

ACKNOWLEDGMENTS

Thanks and appreciation go to my excellent beta-readers, Suzi, Grizelda, and Fran whose suggestions vastly improved the novel from the first draft. Karen Badger and Barbara Bliss of Badger Bliss Books have done another superb job in helping me bring this book to publication, by providing some key edits, formatting the manuscript and creating the cover. I couldn't do it without you.

A Girl on the Plane

Table of Contents

Prologue

High on a Welsh Hill.

"Do you think we will ever come back up here again?"

A light wind from the west was ruffling the branches of the trees behind the cottage, and clouds were chasing each other across the wintry Welsh landscape. Bryony Morris looked back at her wife of only four days as she pushed the second of their suitcases into the back of the hired two door Nissan, and pulled the passenger seat forward into position.

She straightened up and stretching out her arms took stock of what still might need doing to vacate the rental property. But she and Isabel had seen to everything. The cottage was clean and tidy, with the water turned off, and the keys put under the third flower pot to the left of the front door. Their short honeymoon was over and they were ready to leave. She almost wanted to cry.

She pulled out her IPhone, the one Isabel had given her for her birthday back in August, and added, "Hey, just let me take a last picture of you by the cottage."

She gently pushed her wife backwards, so she could catch her framed against the white-washed walls of the old Welsh longhouse.

"Stand there! Now, stop pulling silly faces at me and just give me one of your sweet smiles."

Isabel obeyed, and smiled, looking as though butter wouldn't melt in her mouth, and then responded to both comments at once.

"Of course we'll come back. Let's book a week for some time in the summer. Now, come over here with your little phone and let's make it a selfie."

She pulled Bryony's slightly taller body towards hers and

put their two heads together, so their cheeks were touching. Bryony turned her phone camera round, held it at arms' length and then pushed the button a couple of times.

"Done." She showed Isabel the images. The little pictures were of two very different faces, one slimmer and somewhat weather-beaten, with Irish good looks, clear blue eyes and a wavy bob of dark hair, and next to it, hers, slightly larger and much younger, hazel-green eyes, beautifully regular strong features and a short mop of honey-coloured hair. Bryony looked at the pictures and sighed with satisfaction.

"One more for the album," she said.

"Well, you've taken quite a few dozen already this week. I hope you have a strong password on that phone, because I can think of quite a few of your photographic efforts which mustn't ever get into the public domain."

"Izzy, those I took of you are just for my private delight, don't worry darling. When I'm stuck on the night shift at St Thomas's through the coming weeks I shall just give myself a treat now and then, and sneak a peek at your beautiful body. We did have a lot of fun though, didn't we, while I was taking those late night shots?"

Isabel laughed, and holding her hand, walked with her across to the car, to begin the drive down to the railway station seven miles away.

She said, "It is a shame you've been called in to provide cover right over Christmas, but I understand. Student doctors are the lowest form of pond-life in the general scheme of things. I am trying my best not to be resentful that we've had to cut our honeymoon back from two weeks to less than one, that's all."

Bryony took the key and sat in the driver's seat. She liked to drive, and Isabel rarely complained. Since the accident which had nearly killed her the previous May, Bel had taken the wheel of a car only when necessary, and she hadn't yet replaced her own vehicle.

Bryony knew Isabel still had flashbacks and nightmares about the accident, and would prefer to remain a passenger, especially as it chimed well with her campaign about making lifestyle changes to cut carbon emissions.

Isabel, or Bel, Bridgford, felt that to be alive at all must include running at least one campaign, and climate change was her current focus. She was known in London as one of the foremost speakers and lobbyists on the subject, and the book she had been writing all summer with Bryony's help had been rushed through to publication in the last month or two. It would be out in the public domain very soon.

As they drove south towards Machynllyth, where they would return the hired car and then take the train back through England, Isabel did what she loved to do, turned slightly to the right and quietly observed the beautiful profile of her adored Bryony, her chosen one, her beloved.

She said nothing, just gazed at the much younger woman, with a look of such ardent affection that Bryony felt embarrassed, and tried to think of something to take Isabel's mind off her.

"Well, once Christmas is over, we will have a few more days free, unless you need to return straight away to work."

"I'll probably put in a few hours a day. It will be peaceful, without the team in. Only Steph Hunter might be there. Now that she's home from West Africa, she may well be using the next few days to catch up with her paperwork."

"Steph is the only one of your staff I haven't met, right? Your senior project officer?"

"Yes, she'd left London for Kinshasa before I returned to London with you in September. In fact, I haven't seen Stephanie myself all year, except on Skype, as I was on Sabbatical since March writing the book and then, well, you know the rest, darling."

"What's she like? She looks great fun in her picture on the *Righteous Anger* website."

"Steph is fun. She's also intelligent, sensitive and physically brave. I would trust her with my life, but maybe not my keys. She's notoriously forgetful, but she's excellent with people, and at managing difficult issues across cultures. She and Alana make a very attractive couple."

"Oh, so she's Alana's significant other, then?" Bryony seemed not to have absorbed the fact that when the cool and beautiful Alana Byrne had attended their wedding, she hadn't simply come as Bel's accountant friend, but as the partner of her absent colleague.

She was ashamed to admit it, but that settled a tiny prickle of jealousy caused by Alana's undoubted 'Ice Queen' good looks, and the fact that she'd attended the wedding alone. Bel had kissed her very fondly at the end of the reception, but maybe this was because she'd felt sorry for her, all alone for three and a half months.

They were now driving into the town, and Bryony's attention turned to remembering the directions back to the local car-hire garage. Isabel however thought about Stephanie and Alana for some minutes more. They were dear friends of hers, and she had known Steph since the younger woman was in her mid- twenties.

Being so happy with Bryony, Bel felt quite evangelistic about marriage, but she worried about those other two. When she'd chatted to Alana briefly at the wedding reception, it was obvious that the woman was wound up as tight as a watch-spring, and missing Stephanie most dreadfully. Isabel wouldn't be surprised if there wasn't going to be an explosion of some sort, now Steph had flown back home, and they were reunited.

She knew she couldn't have tolerated being apart from Bryony for three days, let alone three months, but Stephanie never said no to any overseas posting or chance of a field trip. Her passport had more stamps in it than Phineas Finn's!

"I promise, I'll introduce you to them both as soon as possible," she said to her wife, and smiled with possessive pride, as Bryony drew up into the parking space by the Railway station, and carefully began to unpack the vehicle.

"And I'll tell you how Steph and Alana first got together. It was quite as exciting as any Hollywood musical. And I had a ringside seat!"

So, as the train started its long journey down through mid-Wales, to Birmingham, and then on the next train to London, Bel told Bryony all about the events three years before which had brought Alana and Steph from enemies to friends, and then much, much, more.

Chapter 1

Away far too long

Ally Byrne came through the door of her south London flat, and saw her girlfriend and flat-mate, Steph Hunter, sprawled out on the sofa, seemingly asleep, with her travel bag and rucksack thrown down on the floor beside her. She coughed, just to make sure.

"Kittens!" announced Steph, with her eyes still closed.

"Kittens?"

"Kittens. The most sought after images on Facebook apparently."

Ally replied with a slight shrug.

"You don't say. Well, I know not to find any kittens on your pages anyway. You're allergic to cats."

"And to cute. Don't forget cute. You know how that sends me up the wall."

"Hmm. Definitely allergic to cute."

Ally stepped over the luggage, and stood in front of Stephanie, willing her to open her eyes and do her the courtesy of looking at her. Her exasperating partner obliged, rubbing her eyes, and then smiling in that devastating way which lit up the room.

"So, hi. It's good to see you. Did you miss me?"

As she spoke, Steph flung her IPad across the sofa and stretched out her arms and legs in a move which made her resemble a cat languidly pulling itself from sleep. Ally could see how genuinely exhausted she must be, having just returned to the UK from more than three grueling months in the Democratic Republic of the Congo.

Steph's hair stood up on end and looked as though it hadn't seen a comb in days, and her clothes were creased and covered in dust. She had obviously collapsed for a few minutes, giving in to the urge to check the internet for any urgent messages, and spend a few moments scrolling through trivia.

Alana Byrne, or Ally, on the other hand, was as neat as a pin and still immaculate in her business suit and high heeled boots. Her journey had been somewhat less challenging, only a short train ride from a large accountancy firm in the City of London.

Their laconic exchange about kittens was typical of the way they often slid cautiously back into their relationship after months apart. Neither of them seemed good at spontaneously showing their emotions without an ice-breaker.

Alana was overjoyed to see Steph had come safely home from Kinshasa in one piece, but couldn't deny she was, as usual, irritated by the way her girlfriend spread herself and her luggage across their sitting room in total ownership.

The enforced separation had been a long fourteen weeks this time, and Ally had been forced into living on her own resources. Tidiness comforted her, chaos did not. She saw all the muddle and wished it didn't annoy her so much.

Stephanie was a woman whose whole lifestyle never seemed to know its rightful boundaries. She liked to live rough even when the way promised to be smooth. She travelled constantly, and she invaded Ally's heart, dreams, bed, and wardrobe with seemingly casual disregard for the mess she left behind whenever she departed again. As she did all the time.

Alana swallowed her pain. Now wasn't the time for nagging. She put out her arms and Steph stood up and went quickly over to her. She helped her pull off her coat and then gave her a big bear hug.

"I have missed you so much, darling. God, I think I'm getting too old for these trips. And the Internet connection was terrible. Sorry I couldn't Skype you more often. If we weren't having a power cut, it was the water that stopped running in the taps, and we were carrying buckets around the compound. The nights were hotter than hell."

"I know. I understand." Alana kissed her warmly, half on the mouth, half on the cheek. They had been together for nearly three years. They were almost family.

She said to Steph. "Go and jump in the shower, and I'll fix a meal. You know you'll feel better once you've eaten."

"Yes, that stale croissant in Brussels airport seems a long time ago."

Then she remembered, "Oh and something really weird happened on the flight home. I want to run it past you and see what you think."

"OK. Over supper. I'll put some pasta on."

"Great, anything but rice."   And Steph dragged her smelly, weary bones into the bathroom, and turned on the shower.

They sat together an hour later on the small terrace behind the flat, enjoying a glass of Tesco's best red together despite the cold night air. Steph, who loved to sit out and listen to the night sounds of London had grabbed the duvet off the bed and wrapped them both up in it against the December frost. A scented candle made by a Ukrainian women's collective gave them a little pool of reflected light. The white artificial birch tree covered with twinkling LED lights which Ally had decorated with small silver balls sparkled in the corner. It was a gesture towards the festive season, very controlled, very minimalistic, but Steph appreciated it. In your face Christmas decorations always made her slightly uncomfortable.

"So what was the problem on the aeroplane from Kinshasa?" asked Alana, looking into the candle light.

"Not so much a problem for me, but something troubling. At the gate, as we went through the security gates to board, in the queue just in front of me was a large Nigerian family, with several children, and a very young Congolese woman in tow, who seemed to be their nanny or maid."

"And you knew this, how?"

"By the general way they treated her, with the haughty disdain with which the wealthy the world over treat their minions. She was carrying most of their hand luggage and seemed to have responsibility for the younger children.

"I know she wasn't Nigerian like the others, because, when she stepped backwards and accidentally fell over me, she apologised in Lingala. I answered in French, and we knew we were at least on the same wavelength, language-wise."

"So? Sadly, haughty employers browbeating minions is a scenario you see everywhere, especially in airports."

"Yes, but when we were airborne and I stood up to use the toilet, this young woman suddenly arrived behind me in the queue, and thrust a small scrap of paper into my hand with a phone number. She whispered in French, "Please, phone my sister, My Sister! Tell her you saw me on a flight to Brussels. Tell her…""

"Then we were thrown apart by the toilet door opening, and I was pushed inside before I could reply. When I emerged, I saw she had returned to her seat in the centre of a row of five, towards the back of the plane. Her employers were all in business class, naturally. I walked back and looked at her with raised eyebrows. I mouthed, "Are you all right?""

"She looked very scared, and I saw a shifty looking guy sitting next to her, who scowled at her. Maybe he was another employee of the family. She just gave a tiny shake of the head and looked away from me, so I took the hint and retreated.

"When we landed in Brussels, there was no sign of her. She may have gone forward to be with the family when they left abruptly from business class. Perhaps they had a quick connection, but I couldn't see them anywhere as we went through to the transit area. So now, I really don't know what to do."

Alana was surprised by this. "Call the number on the scrap of paper, obviously."

"Well, obviously, duh. But there's no country code. Where is it, in Belgium, the Congo, somewhere on the continent? I tried the basic number as soon as we were off the plane, but they said, "This number does not exist. Please check and dial again.""

"Give it over to me. Let me look at it."

Steph pulled the number out of her IPhone wallet and passed it across. It was on the squared paper, universally used in francophone countries, in ballpoint pen, and had nine numbers.

Steph continued, "It's a puzzle, and it worries me. I can't get her face out of my mind. She looked both exhausted and terrified, and I am sure now she was even younger than I had first thought."

"Have you tried Googling it?"

"Yes. It's not a complete number. I think it lacks a country code. As it is, it's just a seemingly random set of numbers. But it may mean a lifeline to this girl. "

"Let me ask at work tomorrow," said Alana. "One of the tech team might crack this. I expect it's quite simple. We should try the D.R.C. first anyway, don't you think? And why don't you call your boss tomorrow? Isabel will know. She knows everything."

Steph shook her head. "Bel won't be back at work yet. She's supposed to be away on her honeymoon until well after Christmas."

"Perhaps, but maybe you could text her. You know what a workaholic she is. I went to her wedding on your behalf by the way. Everyone we know was there, and they all asked why you weren't present and where were you? I told them you had to stay on in DRC to wind everything up."

"Yes, I was sorry to miss the wedding. I adore Bel, and definitely want to get to know Bryony. We should have them around for a meal in the New Year."

Alana smiled and nodded. It would be a really positive new start if Stephanie could stay in the UK long enough to issue invitations and still be there to honour them.

"Anyway, this mystery phone number, I'll help you sort it out, don't worry."

Steph was clearly grateful Ally was taking it seriously, but the hour was late, and both of them were exhausted. They retreated back into the warmth, left the paper on the kitchen table, turned their wine glasses upside down in the sink, next to the unwashed supper dishes, and fell into bed.

Alana curled around Steph like a spoon behind her back, slowly rubbing her shoulder with one hand and cupping her left breast with the other, but Steph was too tired to respond in any sexual way. She mumbled an apologetic, "love you, Night…" and promptly fell asleep.

There was so much she needed to talk to Steph about, serious stuff, but it would just have to wait now until the following evening. Stephanie was never good in the morning, and Alana needed her full attention and most positive mood if she was to respond well to what she had to suggest. It was perhaps the most important decision they needed to take in their lives, and she desperately wanted Steph to agree to her plan and say "Yes."

"Story of my life," muttered Alana. "In bed with a sleeping beauty," and turned over, hugged her pillow and decided to follow her into the land of Nod. But Alana was going through inner turmoil, and what really scared her, was that she suspected Steph hadn't even noticed.

Chapter 2

Righteous Anger.

When Stephanie woke the following morning, the city sky was still dark, but that didn't mean Alana hadn't left for work more than an hour earlier, hurrying as usual through the wet cold streets of Brixton. The short December days in London meant that the sun hardly rose before 9 am, and it would be setting again by 4 pm. The bright, hot sunshine of West Africa already seemed a fading dream.

Stephanie lay back on the pillows and did a small calculation. It was December 20th, only five days until Christmas, just one until the shortest day, and she had bought no presents, written not a single card, nor even asked Alana what her plans, well, their plans presumably, were for the holiday week coming up.

She knew they had a lot of catching up to do. Alana hadn't said much, but the previous evening she'd sported the same wistful look which had been on her face back in early September. It was a look which had lodged in Steph's mind all the months she'd been absent, and it didn't reassure her now to still glimpse it.

The cause of it, while Steph wasn't totally sure, must include the fact that their relationship, once so sparky and explosively exciting, had been in heading steadily towards the doldrums for ages. And Steph knew ninety percent of the reason lay at her feet. In their scuffed leather boots, they had taken her away from Alana far too often.

She and Alana were so different, like a fish and a bicycle, but they had always complemented each other. They had worked. People even called them the perfect couple.

One of them was extrovert, the other definitely introvert,

one spontaneously reckless, the other cautiously forensic, and one was someone who generally flung doors wide open before thinking what might be behind them. Her partner, however, was someone who never left a room without closing up the windows and checking the locks.

Alana always remembered exactly where Steph had left her keys, her passport, her purse, the many vital pieces of information she'd neglected to write down. Steph loved Alana dearly, and by God she needed her, but she was growing a little weary of the frequent look of slight disappointment on her partner's face.

Alana couldn't say she hadn't known what she was taking on from the beginning. The world in which Steph lived and breathed was rough and tough, and she thrived in it. She was good at her job, which she knew few could do with such good grace and skill, and she sensed the next few years were only going to get more intense. No way was she giving it up to do an office based job like Ally's.

The digital display on their bedside clock clicked over to 08.55. Steph had to be out of bed by 9.00. She must go to the office. Her work in-box would be overwhelmed with emails, debriefing and sharing with her colleagues the challenges and triumphs she'd encountered in Kinshasa might take two hours or longer, and then she had to squeeze in some time to go Christmas shopping.

Steph closed her eyes for the last precious two minutes before her self-imposed alarm (for in reality no-one at work expected her in today) and promised she'd be out of bed in a flash.

Then everything went black. It was 11.30 before she woke again.

Horrified when she saw the time, she made more progress at her second attempt to start the day, took a quick hot shower, brushed back her tawny hair, and pulled on her normal outfit for a winter's day in London. Steph virtually lived in Rohan sports' wear, and today found a set of base layer silk underwear, a lined pair of winter trekkers, and a couple of fleeces. She realized she needed proper insulation against the cold. Her body wasn't used to it. She exchanged her beloved stubby leather boots though for cross-trainers, easier to run in through London.

Her black padded jacket fitted snugly over the whole ensemble and she grabbed her phone and her urban messenger bag as she left the flat. There was no time to eat anything, so she hoped maybe she could grab a coffee on the way to the office, but she needed to make tracks.

Only when she was halfway down the road towards Brixton tube station did Steph remember the paper with the vital phone number she'd left on the kitchen table. But she hadn't seen it there before she left, so with luck, Alana had picked it up. Ally, with her eye for detail, and a photographic memory for numbers, maybe she'd find out how to call the number and relay the young African girl's message to her sister.

To understand the intricacies of the London tube system wasn't rocket science, but some mental block inside Steph's brain, especially after a prolonged absence, often caused her to get into stupid trouble about it. Far too often, she'd end up on the wrong platform for the Northern Line, or overshoot a station while deeply involved in a podcast, and find herself heading out to the wilds of Essex. Her London Underground system dyslexia was weird, as she could navigate across a trackless waste in Outer Mongolia without any trouble, (as she had done once, in her twenties).

Anyway, this morning she decided to take a chance and take route B to the office. One stop on the Victoria Line from Brixton, change at Stockwell, and then catch the Northern Line northeast to Old Street. The three-minute gap between trains in the rush-hour had now stretched to twelve and she realized by the absence of passengers on the platform in the grey tunnel that she must have just missed a train by seconds.

While she waited, Steph rummaged in her purse for some change and went over to a vending machine. Chocolate, glorious chocolate, not a square had passed her lips in fourteen long weeks. She went for the gooiest bar she could see, one with peanuts to raise the protein level a little, and pressed the buttons with its code. The satisfying little clunk as the bar dropped into the retrieval pit gave her a ridiculous amount of joy. The trappings of western civilisation did have their advantages after all!

When her journey by tube finally finished, Steph was sufficiently fortified to run up and out of the station and then walk very briskly the few hundred yards to the crowded and somewhat shabby office block which housed her organization. The agency had once been a paternalistic old fashioned charity, set up by one or two evangelical clergymen in the 1960s with a mission to stop world hunger, hence the unusual name of *"Righteous Anger"*.

However, when Bel Bridgford had swept in as its new CEO five years earlier, she had changed everything. The anger was still there though, in shovelfuls, but they were all too busy to sit around feeling righteous. It was now a woman-led, and women focused, organization, and earned its bread and butter by campaigning.

The current themes were support for homeless women and street-children, working for the abolition of female genital mutilation, and supporting communities affected by climate change. Bel led on the climate change campaign, Steph was the senior project officer and programme manager for street children and homeless women, and their colleague Trixie Nabieu from Sierra Leone was the feisty manager on FGM.

Righteous Anger's rickety infrastructure was kept afloat, just, by their very cool and media-savvy Head of Funding, Caroline Patel. She had come to work with them after a career as a presenter on day-time TV, but still looked and sounded like the elegant newsreader she had been in her twenties. Caroline's background was Gujarati, by way of her great grandparents' exodus from the Indian sub-continent to Uganda in the 1920s, and her parents' subsequent flight to the UK when the Asian middle classes were kicked out of East Africa in early 1972.

Caroline had been born the last of her family's children, in 1965, and could still remember the hot, privileged life they'd all enjoyed in Soroti, a dusty but lively little town where her father had once been manager of a local bank. But life in the UK had also been good to her, and the only thing she now seemed to find useful to remember from her African childhood was a good working knowledge of Swahili, and a fondness for groundnut and cassava leaf stew, and curried goat.

This was a meal she would often cook for Steph and Alana if they ventured way out west to her leafy avenue in Wimbledon. Steph considered Caroline the god-mother of their relationship, as she had smoothed the way for them to fall in love.

That had been an improbable tale from the start, but Steph knew without Caroline's mentoring, she'd still be a miserable singleton, prowling round the few gay clubs and women's haunts which still existed in London. Or using a lonely hearts club online. Everything was online now. If you weren't already part of a couple, real-life in London for a middle-aged gay woman was getting drearier by the day.

These thoughts and memories propelled Stephanie up three flights of stairs and through the door, finally, to her place at work just as the sandwich guy arrived bearing a huge basket of food choices for lunch.

"Hey, you're back!" grinned Jerry, their latest staffer, who looked about twelve, but was an economics graduate from Manchester desperate to get into development work. He was answering the phones and dealing with the mail as usual, in his checked trousers and red jersey. Bel had nicknamed him Rupert Bear early on in his placement, and when the younger staff and he had looked it up, the tag had stuck. He was a campy little guy, unfazed by working for an agency which contained a veritable tribe of lesbians.

"Hi, Rupes, where is everybody?"

Steph chose a large triple-decker sandwich from their visitor, and paid for it with the remaining change from her journey home. Then she went over to her desk. Even by her normal standards, clearing it up would be a challenge, with the wooden desktop covered with three months' worth of junk mail, magazines and folders.

She visibly quailed at the sight of it, and Rupert/Jerry hastily apologized.

"I honestly didn't expect you back before Christmas. I was going to go through it and sort it into piles for you."

"Where is everyone else?"

"They've all gone down to Water Conservancy Brigade HQ

on the first floor. There's a drinks party for Christmas. But they'll be back up here before long I expect."

"Do you want to go down and join them? It would be good for you to network. I can answer the phone if it rings."

"Thanks, Steph. I will. And I'll tell them you're here. I'm sure they'll want to bring you up to speed with everything which has happened since you left."

Jerry didn't elaborate, but Steph wondered whether he was meaning anything in particular, apart from perhaps the miraculous transformation in their brilliant CEO's fortunes and well-being.

Apparently, Bel's sabbatical year, which had been such a disaster in the beginning, had ended spectacularly by her marrying a woman seventeen years her junior. Stephanie had not even met Bryony in person, but a picture of the honeymooners in Wales had just popped up on Instagram.

Steph and Bel went back a long time in the aid sector, from long before Bel had recruited her back in 2015. Steph had been there through the final years of Bel's volcanic partnership with Carrie Monterini, and then through the catastrophe of Carrie's murder.

She wanted the very best for her old friend and boss, and the sudden appearance of Bryony in Bel's life seemed totally positive. Bel's face on the screen, when they had been able to get through to each other by Skype, had been wreathed in smiles. She looked ten years younger than she had back in May, even before she had had that devastating car-crash.

But there was no doubt now, after the latest general election the previous week, Bel, Caroline, and Festus, their Head of Finance, would need all their wits about them, and a large helping of good luck on top, to save the agency from financial collapse.

They relied on EU funding for at least a third of their income, and the anti-European sabre-rattling which had gone on for the last two years had been very damaging.

Jerry disappeared off to the party, diverting calls to Steph's phone and she sat down at her desk by the window. The office was chilly and she kept her jacket on. But before tackling the mail, she pulled out her phone and called Alana. Even top-flight

CPAs surely allowed themselves tiny lunch-breaks.

As she ripped open the sandwich package, she started to speak to her loved one.

"Hi. Babe, did you pick up the phone number paper when you left? You did? Great. Yes, I slept in…eleven-thirty in the end…can you read me out the number? I'm going to give it to Rupert to research. He seems rather under-employed and bored here at the moment…Thanks."

They then started a conversation about who was fetching food for supper, and what time they'd both be home. But Steph changed the direction of the discussion.

"Look, why don't we meet here in town? I haven't bought a single card or a present yet, and if we're going north together tomorrow to see our aged Ps, it's our only chance."

Alana sounded a little surprised that she expected them to do their normal routine for Christmas, which was to visit both families in a flurry over the weekend before, so they could spend the actual Christmas Day together.

There was a catch in her voice even. But she said she'd love to connect up for supper in town. They agreed to meet at 5.45 pm at the entrance to Covent Garden tube station, which was a gateway to all sorts of delightful little cafes and shops, and outdoor stalls that would no doubt be loaded with possible present ideas.

Steph closed her phone. Ally had sounded in her normal work-mode, her sensible and calm self. She also said she had asked her assistant to try to identify the source of the mystery phone number, so by the end of the day, with two bright young things working on the case, they might hopefully have an answer.

With only a few days before Christmas, Steph felt keenly for the girl on the plane, and for her sister, somewhere out there in the world, probably worried sick about her.

But now, she had work to do, with the need to make a semblance of order on her poor little desk! She finished the sandwich, threw the wrapper accurately into the waste-bin from twelve feet away, brewed herself a much-needed fairly-traded mug of instant coffee, and sat down to the task.

She absolutely did not share Jerry's optimism that all her co-workers would come back any time soon. Christmas parties just didn't work like that. But he was only twenty-one. He'd learn!

Chapter 3

A mind like a gimlet.

Two miles away as the crows, should they care to make the trip, might choose to fly, in her glass-plated office in the City, Alana was trying to redirect her thoughts to the task at hand, making sense of a very complicated set of spreadsheets on which her junior colleagues had admitted defeat.

Her accountancy firm, or at least the large section she headed, concentrated on high-end corporate fraud in the banking sector. Their prey within the criminal fraternity of dodgy accountants and confidence tricksters had world-class skills in money laundering and hiding illegally acquired cash in plain sight, and it was her task to beat them at their own game.

In the seventeen years since she had passed her CPA exams and cut her teeth on conducting endless audits for publically listed companies, Alana had certainly perfected her skills of tracking. She had the tenacity of a terrier, and a mind like a gimlet, coupled with occasional flashes of inspired intuition, and it was these abilities and forensic attention to detail which had already exposed some major scandals which had rocked the City of London in recent years.

More than one major finance house had gone to the wall as a result of Alana Byrne exposing malpractices at the highest level, and she didn't take kindly to being fobbed off with wince-making comments like, "Come along little lady"… or "Don't you worry your pretty little head…" which had plagued her in her twenties. With Alana, the cover was definitely not the book, as foolishly condescending crooks soon learned to their cost.

Approaching forty, she was now at the top of her game, and her cool grey eyes, looking out from under the ash-blonde bob she still maintained as her default hairstyle, could instantly see subtle deceptions in a spreadsheet full of formulae which few others might notice.

In her late twenties Alana had spent five years in the Treasury. However, the monotony of directly working for the government had finally made her decide to return to the private sector, headhunted by a firm of investigative accountants who worked independently under contract to the British Government and other international bodies like the World Bank.

But Alana hid a radical heart under her smart suits and expensive haircuts. Her father had been a dockworker in his youth, and she came from a raucously argumentative Manchester family. She'd been brought up in a terraced house close to Salford Docks, and her parents still lived in the area. Alana could slip out of her Oxford accent, back into a Manchester twang if the occasion required, and was fiercely loyal to her roots, as well as always supporting any under-dog which trotted past.

Meeting (well, confronting might be a better word) Stephanie when she had been asked to supervise the auditing of Righteous Anger's accounts, had been the turning point of both Alana's professional and personal life. She had fallen in love so dramatically, and at the time, she had thought, so disastrously, that for a while her head hadn't stood a chance against the rampaging passions of her heart.

The return fire from this new exasperating, glorious person in her life had been as intense as hers was, and they had fallen together into the furnace. Her Ins were Steph's Outs. They fitted together like two diametrically opposed jigsaw pieces. And their fit was considered perfect.

But now, having connected, and shared a flat and a bed for three years, she felt they were like trains stuck in a siding. They weren't going anywhere. They almost just co-existed, compared to the early days of their love affair, and Alana had let it lie like that for too long.

She had real needs, and she knew she should express them, and then like a real catalyst during this last three-month separation, she'd been given an offer which no sensible person in her situation could afford to ignore. It involved a high six-figure package as Chief Finance Officer for one of the world's largest aid agencies' with a budget in the hundreds of millions of dollars, but it would mean a relocation to New York, and this she knew would mean in essence the death of her relationship with Steph.

She may have been head-hunted, but to Alana, it felt almost like the head-hunters of Polynesia were after her scalp. She doubted if she would survive alone without Steph, whom she loved so dearly.

But hadn't Steph, by her repeated actions, or inaction, down-graded their partnership herself? She foresaw her own heart breaking if they split up, but Steph had never indicated it would break hers. The recruitment agency wanted to set up an interview for her with members of the Board of *Financial International Resource for Emergencies*, or *FIRE*, immediately after the Christmas holidays, on January 3rd to be precis. She had the next two weeks to decide what to do, to go for the job, or not, and to tell Stephanie about it, or not. The dilemma was frying her brain.

So while she employed part of her mind in tracking down the missing millions in a balance sheet, she was also processing Steph's phone call, and how to plan a strategy for the coming holiday period.

Christmas was always fraught for Stephanie, whose parents' divorce still left an open wound at the centre of her family, so she was usually hyper-jumpy, quick to burst into tears, or sometimes equally wanting to behave outrageously and be almost sick with excitement. Steph's mother had never done Christmas well, so whether they spent it with her, or tried to go somewhere else, her misery usually dampened any festive cheer they might muster.

Alana's own family usually simply ate too much and then got drunk on public holidays, apart from her sweetheart of a Muslim brother-in-law, who would join Steph and her on the backdoor step for left-wing debates about the future of Palestine, and the latest troubles in Kashmir.

A tap came on the door, and Karen, her PA, put her head around.

"Sorry to disturb, but we've done some work on those numbers you gave us."

"Oh, yes? Please, come in. Any success?"

"The computer says there could be a digit missing, besides a country code, but we have five options it seems."

"Tell me."

"One might be a mobile phone network number in Congo Brazzaville, if you add a 7."

"Possible. That is likely."

"One could be in Russia."

"Unlikely, don't you think? The girl was definitely West African."

"O.K. Well then two could be French numbers, again with missing digits, perhaps 4 or 5 at the end, and one we think could be for a landline in Canada, in the Montreal area. You wouldn't need extra numbers for that, just the country code."

Alana took the printout from her assistant's hand.

"Thanks Karen. Well done. You and the computer have both been very clever. I'll show these to Steph and we'll compare notes. I'm meeting her later up West."

Then she had another idea. "Can you do some research for me on modern-day slavery, especially about young girls from sub-Saharan Africa? See if there are any up-to-date stats. About it. Oh, and ask Brian to come here, will you? I think I may have found the missing millions he was chasing."

Karen beamed. She loved to please, and her secret crush on her elegant, brilliant boss had just received a warm boost. She went off happily to summon their colleague.

It was four-thirty before the Righteous Anger staff team rolled back into their offices, and the sky outside was already dark. Steph had spent the last few hours productively clearing her desk and writing up her reports about the street-kids' project in Kinshasa.

She had secured funding for a new rescue centre for girls, and had gone to sign off on the project, which in practical terms had meant she stayed to accompany the local team while they constructed the building and staffed it. It was a new venture for a project which had previously only catered for boys, but the ever-growing numbers of homeless kids living rough meant that girls badly needed their own facilities.

While there were fewer girls than boys living rough around the world, Steph knew only too well how vulnerable they were, and constantly at risk of trafficking and exploitation. Unlike the boys' centre which was only a day-time drop-in centre, offering a range of vital services like schooling, washing and laundry, medical care, and counselling, but ultimately closing its doors every day at 5 pm, the girls' house was residential.

Even more importantly, it had a security guard to keep out night-time intruders. Twenty girls, aged six to fourteen, could be accommodated under the care of a team of professionally trained women, and the trauma and sexual abuse most of them had already experienced made it intense work.

Steph wrote up her notes, and downloaded and filed her photos. She wished Isabel was there to debrief her. There had been so many issues, so much anger in her at the plight of the little girls, which she needed to unload onto someone else. And there was no-one better than Bel for helping her process the intensity of her field-trips, and suggest practical actions to take her findings forward.

But she knew her boss would be now sinking deeper into a lovely honeymoon over Christmas. She'd be back in a week's time, and they could have a meeting then. "Patience!" Steph told herself. "You're still on a high from all the travel. Calm down. Deep breaths. Get into the Christmas spirit."

Then the door burst open and the gang were back from their party. Trixie, Caroline and Festus all grinned broadly as she rose to greet them as they returned to their desks. Festus was the token man in their team, and also fitted his stereotype of a Finance Manager by being the only member of staff to wear a jacket and tie, gave her a warm hug.

He had been born on the island of St Vincent sixty years earlier, and still had a slight Southern Caribbean lilt to his accent, which otherwise was pure South London. He'd spent his childhood less than a mile from where she and Alana now had their flat and had stayed loyal to his roots, just moving further out of central London to where he could raise his kids with a garden, and grow vegetables.

Festus was relatively new to the agency, having been brought in as a qualified accountant after the disastrous exposure of fraud which Alana, in her role as a new auditor for their books had discovered on her first visit. Ally had come in at Bel's invitation, after the new CEO had made horrifying discoveries in virtually her first week on the job, and Festus's appointment had been one great positive to come out of that time of trauma.

Steph viewed financial matters almost with the same degree of cautious apprehension with which she viewed the map of the London underground system. Her first degree had been in peace studies, and her masters' degree in international relations, so keeping accounts had never been the favourite section of her job description. Now she was delighted Festus ran the books for her projects, and Caroline did all the budgeting and secured her enough grants to run them.

Caroline, who sat just behind her in their crowded office, was packing her things to go home. Realistically, no-one would be wanting a lobbying phone-call from her late on Friday, December 20th.

Steph swivelled her chair round to talk to her before she left.

"Sorry, I'm back to spoil your view through the window?"

"Ha, no problem. It's good to see you."

"Are you taking the whole week as leave?"

"Yes, well officially the offices will be shut anyway until after New Year's Day. It will be the same in Africa, and in the States and Europe. No-one will work now until mid-January."

"Going anywhere warm?"

"Yes, Charlie and I are off to Cancun, but don't tell anyone."

Stephanie knew that Charlie's given name was Charlotte. She was a North London Jewish comedienne Caroline had met when she worked for ITV, half Caroline's height, twice her width, and the love of her life.

Their relationship remained a closely guarded secret, not least from Caroline's elderly parents who were perpetually sad for her, that she had never married and therefore must be completely lonely and loveless. At least both Steph and Alana's families knew all about their relationship, even if they had caused problems about it at the start. It was ridiculous that Caroline, a sophisticated woman of fifty-five, still felt she had to hide who she was from her parents.

"Well, have a ball. I've been out in the sun too much to envy you, but you'll need some Vitamin D."

Steph then told Caroline and Trixie who had returned as well, all about the girl on the plane.

"I'll feel really bad if I can't help her, contact her sister at least."

"Yes, with it being Christmas and all," mused Trixie. Her mind was obviously full of the need to collect her children from their childminder and pick up supper ingredients as well.

"If I have any ideas which might help, I'll text you. Otherwise, see you on January 2nd. 'Bye now. I'm so glad you stayed safe. None of that Ebola re-emerging at least?"

"No, not in Kinshasa, only in the east of the country. Thank God."

And Trixie had left.

Caroline thought about Steph's remarks about the girl and said. "It's an intriguing story. If you solve the mystery over Christmas, we could write it up for the January newsletter. As Trixie's said, if I have any ideas, I'll text you. Best of luck."

One by one, the post-party gang of four left the office. Only Jerry/Rupert remained after 5 pm, when he approached Steph with a list of possible locations for the phone number. His computer had suggested Congo Brazzaville, Montreal and Moscow.

"That's something to start with. I think there's a digit missing somewhere. Sorry I'm not more use."

Steph pushed her fingers back through her hair, and stretched her arms high behind her head. She should make an appointment to have it cut. In the past three months it had grown down well over her collar and was frankly a mess.

"No, you've been great. I'll try these on Ally and see what she says. Now you get off as well. And Happy Christmas, Jerry.

See you next year!"

Jerry put on a Rupert Bear like duffle coat and disappeared into the early evening rush hour. Alone once again in the office, Steph had a sudden feeling of pre-Christmas anguish. It was just the time of year her father had walked out twenty years before, when she was thirteen, almost casually letting slip that he'd had a second secret family for five or more years already, and was now going to join them permanently.

This bolt from the blue had sent her mother spiralling down into a depression from which she'd never fully recovered. It had also rather taken the gilt off the gingerbread for their family for every single Christmas season thereafter.

However, for the last two years, her mother had at least agreed to spend Christmas day with Steph's younger brother Craig and his family. He and his wife Jan had two undeniably adorable young children.

"My only comfort," their granny would say, as she hugged the toddlers, which made Steph feel she'd definitely underperformed as a daughter. Stephanie rescuing babies from the streets of Kinshasa didn't count as an especially comforting thought, obviously.

Steph's mood lightened, however, as she pulled herself together, packed her bag, and turned off the office lights, before locking the door. She was going to meet Ally, and the very thought of her girlfriend raised her libido along with her spirits.

Alana was show-stoppingly gorgeous, and not only to Steph who always had a fatal weakness for Ice Queen Cool. She vowed when they met in town, she would wine and dine her lover, and take the sad faraway look from her eye. Yes, some mulled wine, and some hot roasted chestnuts, and she was sure she could warm Alana up! She just had to remember the right train changes for Covent Garden tube station, always a tricky little destination.

Chapter 4

Christmas shopping.

When Steph emerged from Covent Garden station half an hour late, just after six-fifteen, Alana was patiently standing there, waiting for her. Darling, faithful, long-suffering Alana, Steph knew she didn't deserve her. She had tried to be early, honestly, but the trains had all been packed, and she'd been prevented from squeezing through to the door the first time her train had drawn into Covent Garden. It seemed everyone in London wanted to get their Christmas shopping done in the market there tonight.

Steph had been forced to go one extra stop to Leicester Square, leap out, run over to the other platform and come back again, standing as close to the door as she could this time so as not to have some bizarre squashing situation happen again. She decided she hated travelling by Tube, absolutely hated it.

She could see Alana was more than chilly, huddled down inside her navy trench coat, her hands in soft leather gloves, and her nose pink in the cold evening air.

"Don't tell me! You overshot the station again."

"Yes, but no way was it my fault this time! I simply couldn't get to the door in time without breaking bones and stepping on several small children. Shall we go and get something to eat and drink first, or do you want to go shopping and risk the queues being even longer in an hour?"

Steph linked her arm in Alana's and kissed her face impulsively. Alana squirmed, but obviously liked it. She replied, "Oh, let's get inside somewhere warm and eat early. The restaurants will only get more crowded the later it gets. Besides, I'm starved. I had no time for anything other than a mug of tea at lunchtime. What about you?"

"I had a sandwich from the delivery guy, but it seems a very long time ago now."

They barrelled their way through the festive crowds and fell over the threshold of one of their favourite restaurants, one which thankfully had opened earlier in the evening than some others, to catch hungry office workers. The French proprietor recognised them both and beckoned them over to a pleasantly dark and cosy corner towards the back.

This was almost like old times. At last, they had an hour or two together to talk properly over a well-cooked meal which someone else was providing. There was so much to say, and their relationship was so important, but where to begin?

As Stephanie watched Alana slowly unwind her long cashmere and silk pashmina, and slip off her navy coat, letting it rest over the back of her chair, the sheer beauty of her lover made her mouth grow dry. Alana was a natural princess. She had style, she had class, and whoever heard she had kicked around the old cobbled streets of Salford in her youth might be forgiven for thinking it couldn't be true.

She had come up from nothing, and yet always looked like a million dollars. Steph, who had been brought up in the lofty white highlands of Fulwood in west Sheffield, and whose father had inherited a million pounds, or something near it, always felt an uncultured scruff beside her.

Steph stared at her now and kicked herself for staying on in West Africa for so long. She realized just how much she had missed Alana. Unlike the White Queen in Alice in Wonderland, who cried before bad things happened, just to save time, Steph suddenly wanted to cry now, realising how lonely she'd been, trying to sleep in her narrow bed under a mosquito net for fourteen weeks alone in a hot little room. Tears filled her eyes.

"What's the matter?" asked Alana, as she opened the menu.

"No...nothing. I just realized how much I've missed you. Sorry."

"Silly old bear," said Alana calmly. "It's probably just low blood sugar. Let's have some bread and tapenade to keep us going. Then I'm having the aubergine parmigiana."

Stephanie picked up her menu.

"Right you are, darling. Here goes then," And she called the waiter over, as her tears dried. Eat first, then talk. It seemed a very good idea. She just hoped she didn't make a spectacle of herself with any more inappropriate weeping.

The food came, along with a bottle of deep red, peppery Cotes du Rhone, and they ate together, savouring the food. Stephanie chose the Cassoulet, one of the restaurant's specialities, and enjoyed the warm stew-like mixture of beans, chicken, sausage, and vegetables as they slid down her throat. The level of wine in the bottle also soon sank down.

Alana watched Steph appreciatively as she tucked in, and almost wished she didn't find her girlfriend's physicality so very alluring. She could watch her for hours, just loving how her body moved, how her strong muscles seemed to glide under that perpetually golden tinged skin. Even watching Stephanie sip wine made her want to clench her legs together in anticipation.

Because she spent more than half the year in the world's hotter countries, Steph never sported the normal British winter pallor, and had the lucky combination of skin which tanned easily along with blue eyes and a honey-coloured mop of hair. She exuded a look of good health, even if in reality she felt seriously unwell. Recurrent bouts of malaria were always a problem.

Alana always fed her soul by looking at her, but now she was definitely feeling undernourished. They were apart so much, and she was getting older. She needed a lover who would be there more of the time, someone in her bed every night, not just now and then. Something had to change in their relationship, urgently if they were to stay together.

But now, as they slowly warmed up and unwound from the stresses of their working days, they turned to the immediate task between them. Alana opened the conversation.

"What did you discover about the phone number from your end?"

"Well, it seems most likely there's a crucial digit missing

somewhere, which is a real bummer, but Jerry came up with five ideas which might work with what we've got. Two French numbers, both in the Paris region, one down in Brazzaville, which was the next-door country to where we both boarded the plane, so that's a good bet, then a wild card in Moscow, and one number, way over in Montreal, Canada. What about your end?"

"Karen missed the French numbers, but otherwise she thinks the same as Jerry. I was also wondering if we couldn't try to identify the girl herself, by trying to access the passenger list on your flight somehow. The airline will have it surely."

"Yes, it will, but isn't that classified information? How could we find out?"

"I'm not sure, just now, but I think there might be ways. Can you remember roughly what her seat number might have been? If we are going to do this, we might as well do a thorough job."

"I know they publish passenger lists after a plane disaster, but I'd think ordinary flights would be kept confidential. Any way of finding out?"

"I could ask a friend of mine who works for Air France. But we may not need to do that. Shall we first work through the possible number combinations we know and call them all?"

"Not now, in this crowded restaurant. It's too noisy and it might be a distressing call for the right person on the other end. But tomorrow, before we leave…"

Alana looked up from her plate. So maybe they would at least be spending Christmas like they used to, doing the rounds of their families as she'd hoped. But she'd learned not to take anything for granted with Steph.

"So, you're thinking…we're still going to see your Mother tomorrow, and Sunday and then move onto Manchester for the next two nights?"

"Of course! Oh Ally, I never imagined we wouldn't. Of course, I need you with me if I'm to survive even one night at home in Sheffield. Have you made any other plans?"

Alana looked into Steph's undeniably 'bedroom' eyes, and gulped, half with pure lust, and half because of her adrenalin telling her she had to clear the air by sharing what might certainly become earth-shattering plans for their relationship.

"No, of course not. I just didn't want to presume anything, without discussing it."

"God damn it, woman, I've come four thousand miles home to spend Christmas with you! Why do you throw these curve balls at me suddenly, as though there's a problem?"

Alana looked into her eyes steadily. She didn't want an argument. She absolutely didn't want a row, not after so many weeks of longing, of sexual frustration and loneliness.

Maybe, after they'd had some good sex, she'd find the right words to say to address bigger issues, the elephants which were beginning to crowd into their room. But she knew what she wanted tonight, and was intelligent enough not to scupper it.

She leaned forward, took Steph's fingers between her own and squeezed them.

"Darling, don't get upset. All I want to do tonight is to get you home and into bed, and then kiss away all the stress and tiredness from your long journey. Are you up for sex now? After a good night's sleep? Because I can tell you, I can't wait."

It was a good job they were in a shadowy corner, so Alana wasn't overheard, nor was the sudden deep red blush which travelled up Steph's cheek visible to anyone but her. She had a huge sense of relief when her fingers were squeezed in return.

"Alana Byrne, you are the sexiest woman in London, and yes, I am sure I can do better at showing you how much I love and appreciate you, much better than last night. Let's dash round all the stalls and do a little Christmas shopping, then take the Tube home. I'll text Mum and let her know not to expect us before tea-time tomorrow, so we can use the morning to try the mystery numbers."

She quietly drew her finger over Alana's palm, making her wriggle with arousal, and held her gaze. Alana breathed in. Maybe this would all be OK. At least now she knew Steph still fancied her. In fact, they fancied each other like old times.

"Brilliant idea. Let's go. I'll pay. Wave the waiter over sweetie and let's move out of here."

***

It was past ten p.m. when the couple finally arrived home at their flat, juggling several bags and parcels between them. After eating, Steph found her second wind for some Christmas shopping, and Alana, confident now that the evening would end in a satisfyingly sexy way, had allowed her to pull them both through the long lines of Christmas themed stalls and little shops.

Between them they soon found something suitable as a gift for all the adult members of both their families, Stephanie, disappearing at one point, said she needed fifteen minutes to get something special for Ally, and then returned with a happy smile on her face but no visible extra parcel in her hand. It must have been something small. They then managed to catch a crowded tube train south to Brixton, at the end of the Victoria line.

Once home, all the presents were soon deposited on the kitchen table, along with the rolls of wrapping paper and tinselled ribbons which Alana had added to the shop. Then they just stood and looked into each other's eyes in the shadowy light of the side lamp.

"Let me run you a bath," whispered Steph quietly, "and then let me join you in the tub. I know you've had a long hard week, and a long few dry months as well."

Alana nodded, with one of those smiles which had the power to turn Steph's insides to mush. "What a sensible idea!" she murmured. Taking off her coat, and hanging it up neatly, she also picked up Steph's jacket from the floor and added it onto the coat rack. Then she turned back, locked their front door, and said, "Lead on MacDuff."

Chapter 5

The Hunter and the Hunted.

Since the very first day they had met, Alana had been the hunted, and Stephanie the hunter. Hunter by name, and hunter by nature. Older by three years, (and by a decade if you measured age lived by experiences of failed lesbian relationships,) of the two she had always been the elusive antelope in the jungle. Steph had been the tracker, the one who had set the traps to lure her in.

In the end, Steph had been forced to thrash her way towards the ice-queen beauty whose heart was well protected by a forest of thorn bushes and preserved in icepacks of impenetrable frostiness. It had been a classic tale of lesbian tropes and amused them both when they thought back about how their romance had started.

However, having caught her woman, Alana could see Stephanie hadn't really known what to do with her, and this was where Alana's experience counted. She had a lot of fun tutoring Steph in how to be a grown-up lesbian, and some weekends they hardly ever left the bedroom.

But after the first six months of mind-blowing sexual capers, when Steph had to go away on her first long trip in their relationship, and then again in a few months on her second, and then her third, they had both seemed to make an unspoken, silent pact not to be so needy, to almost not love each other too fiercely. It simply made the separations less traumatic, more manageable. And Alana always was a good manager.

She carried on, month after month, holding down her highly responsible and demanding job. She paid the costs of their comfortable flat, cooked all her own meals and ate them in solitude, went out with friends when invited, and she never cried in public.

But now she knew she was almost approaching a breakdown. Attending Isabel and Bryony's wedding on her own, making excuses for Steph's absence, even for one of Bel's oldest friends and closest colleagues, this had been the last straw. Things had to change, or she had to leave. A relocation to New York might be just the answer. Something had to give. They were in a crisis, surely Steph felt it too?

But tonight, oh, tonight Stephanie was being her sweetest, most beguiling, most domestic darling, and Alana simply arched her back like a cat and let herself be loved.

When she heard the taps running for a deep and relaxing bath, she could also smell the Molton Brown tiger lily essence which Stephanie was pouring in to make a real spa experience. She stood in the centre of their bedroom, and began to take off her clothes, kicking her boots away, and then sitting on the end of the bed to unpeel herself from all her winter city clothes.

"Let me," whispered Steph. Coming to Alana, she held her by the jacket lapels, kissed her mouth and then removed her garments, layer by layer.

"You…are…so…beautiful," she whispered, punctuating each word with a kiss, as she undid Alana's shirt buttons.

"So are you," replied Alana, as she allowed the undressing to get even more efficient. Steph's branded Rohan fleeces, her 'uniform', would have to come off as well, but for now, she was passive, letting herself be stripped down to her bra and panties.

She knew Steph always got a kick out of doing it, doing what no-one else was ever allowed to, and the unabashed worshipping which went with the process couldn't fail to please. Pretending to be a gay goddess for a little while never did a girl any harm after all.

Undressing them both took longer than ten minutes, and Steph had had to rush through to the bathroom to turn off the taps before the water rose too high halfway through. They finally stood together shivering naked in their bedroom, not from cold, as the thermostat had been turned up to maximum, but from arousal, and each could feel the frisson of electricity sparking between them.

They moved slowly towards each other and Alana ran her

hands over Stephanie's body, down her breasts, and loved the way her nipples immediately hardened with desire. Stephanie, with much bolder manners, went straight between Ally's legs and rubbed her hand slowly upwards, feeling the soft short curls of Alana's blonde pubic hair as she delved inside, her fingers slippery with Ally's arousal.

"Let's take that bath," she said, "Before the water cools."

They lay back in the delicious heat together, Alana behind, with Steph cradled between her legs, and she pulled her head back against her, so she could nibble and kiss her ears, and whisper sweet nothings. The long, long separation was finally over. They were melding together again, as one. It felt wonderful.

A long day, a bottle of wine, deep water and some definite mutual affection held them in the bath-tub until they nearly fell asleep, but then Steph remembered just how much she enjoyed reducing Alana to a gibbering wreck of womanhood, and pulled the plug out with her toe. She leaped out the bath, grabbed their towels, and hauled Alana to her feet.

"Bed, Princess. Now."

"Yes, Ma'am."

Alana wrapped a bath-sheet round and round her body, but then unwound it again, discarded it, and obediently lay down naked on their bed. Her hair had managed to stay relatively dry, but the ends were wet against her collar-bones, and her skin was damp with a mixture of anticipation and the steam from the bath.

Stephanie came towards her with a look not unlike a saucy pirate's. When she was in the mood for sex, she was unstoppable, and shedding her own towel she fell on Alana and took complete control.

She had larger breasts than Alana's, and they now seemed to have a vitality of their own, swinging above Alana's mouth as she futilely tried to catch one between her teeth.

But soon there was no chance for any retaliatory action. Stephanie had Alana at her mercy, and began a rhythmic pulse with her three fingers, back and forth over her clit and up into the dark and secret passage behind. Within very few minutes she could feel herself bringing her to orgasm smoothly and easily.

Alana's face was damp with sweat and her eyes were closed. Then she let out a low moan and almost swallowed Steph's hand inside her. "Oh, please, stop, stop now!" Steph could feel her whole body pulsing in orgasm against her, and pulling Alana's hair back so her head lifted, she covered her mouth with a powerful, almost biting kiss, invading her mouth with her tongue and owning her.

Alana grabbed the hand which had been doing such wicked things inside her, and pulled it up. Then she sucked on the fingers, tasting herself, making the connection complete. She felt Steph wrap herself round her, grabbing her ass now and putting her thigh between her legs. Alana let herself be hugged, let Steph's sexual power light them both up. It was a wonderful, liberating feeling, the connection between them.

It took a little while, but when Alana had recovered her senses and her heart-rate dropped to a respectable rate of pounding inside her chest, she used her own skills to get at least one scream out of Steph. She knew what excited her lover more than anything, and began by the feather-light breathing into her ear, along with dancing fingers and then lightly scratching fingernails over her back.

It wasn't so much of the "Wham, bam, thank you Ma'am" approach, as the slow building up of unbearable tension throughout Steph's insides, until Alana's sweet tongue and neat little teeth worked their magic, dropping unexpected kisses and then cheeky little bites against the soft skin of her inner arms, her thighs, and then a quiet little lick or two against her labia. Steph seemed to be enduring it as long as she could, but then she came roaring out of the tunnel as if she was aboard a fun-fair roller-coaster cresting to the top of the ride.

Alana hoped Steph was realising how much she needed this, how much they both did. God, her lover was such an idiot for staying away so often. Why had she denied them both this wonderful sex for so long? They were made for each other. They worked so well, fitted together perfectly, and they fancied each other like mad, still.

She finally wrapped her girl-friend up in her arms and

smoothed Steph's untamed locks away from her face before giving her one last deep kiss on her mouth. A distant church clock chimed midnight, and they fell asleep together within seconds of each other. If it wasn't a solution to any of their underlying problems, their sex life was certainly powerful therapy and wonderful leisure activity for a winter's night.

Chapter 6

Wrong numbers and strange conversations.

"Where do we start?"

"With the Brazzaville Congo number, that's the most likely."

They were both curled up in their dressing gowns clutching mugs of coffee on the sofa the following morning. Alana had the list of possible locations for the phone number from her office and handed the phone over to Steph.

"You do it. Your French is much better than mine."

"OK, now let's work out time zones. West Africa will be fine right now. Here goes. But look up the country code for me, will you?"

When that was established, she dialled through, hoping that someone would pick up. But they were both disappointed. It was a business number, some import/export company and a recorded message said the offices would reopen after Christmas, not until January 6th. It seemed that the Congolese like many people south of the Sahara took their main annual vacation break over Christmas and New Year.

When she listened to the crackly message, Steph realized there was nothing sensible she could leave as her reply. She stopped the phone and looked at Alana.

"What can we say? Ask if there's someone there who has a sister who works for some Nigerians. Without her name, this is going to be very difficult."

"Hmm. Well, keep trying. How about Moscow. They are well ahead of us, and their Christmas holidays won't be starting any time soon. Give them a go. At least you can eliminate them."

"Ha, well you can do it. Your Russian is no better than

mine, so we can only try in English."

They went through the same procedure, and Alana waited for someone to respond. The phone was answered, and something unintelligible in Russian was spoken. "Do you speak English?" asked Alana, which seemed the most sensible opening to the conversation. "Niet," was the answer, and the phone was promptly put down.

"Well, that went well. We must sound like idiots. We must find someone who is Russian speaking to make that call. Who do we know?"

"Phil Cooper. I knew him at Bradford Uni. He's heavily into Russian. He edits a magazine looking at global conflict resolution and peace-making. He'd help us, I'm sure."

"So where does he live?"

"He teaches at Sheffield University, so he must live someone near there. When we go up this afternoon, I'll look for him. I expect he's online."

"But the university will have closed for the holidays. It may not be at all easy."

"Phil's a great networker. I expect he's all over social media. It would be good to see him again after all these years. It must be twelve years since we graduated together."

"Right. So a bit of a lead. Try the French numbers next."

Stephanie did, but what might have been a straightforward solution turned out to be very disappointing. One number, with an added 7 for luck, was a pet-grooming salon south of Paris, where the owner sounded rather indignant that she'd know any West African girl, "Not round here," she said firmly. "How did you even get this number?"

"I'm sorry," replied Steph, "wrong number," and closed down that call.

"We can't just stick random digits in. It's crazy," said Alana. "We're simply wasting time and money."

"I'll have one last go with the other French number. Rupert suggested putting a zero after the area code."

The random person who answered the next call was certainly much more pleasant and said she could fit them in for a table at 9 pm that evening. (It must be a popular restaurant.) But she knew no young Congolese girl, the only Africans she knew were Moroccan men, running a bistro down the street.

So that was that, and the only remaining possible lead was a Canadian number, somewhere near Montreal.

"They are five hours behind us. We can't call now. It will be four in the morning still."

"A job for later then. Now, make us both a fresh pot of coffee, and I'll sit at the table and wrap all these presents."

Steph certainly didn't argue with that idea. Alana was the perfect present wrapper, while she was completely hopeless. She couldn't even undo a roll of sticky tape without falling into furious tears of frustration.

"Would you like one of those coffee pod gadgets for Christmas, she asked. "They seem all the rage."

"No sweetie. Far too expensive, and ecologically appalling. All that aluminum for one little cup and they come out at about 28 pence a shot. I still love my old cafetiere."

Alana collected her scissors and ruler, tape and paper, and sat down to complete the present wrapping. She measured every parcel and cut the paper exactly to fit. It was almost Japanese, the art-form she made of it. Steph saw it as a small illustration of how conservative she was with all her resources.

If they hadn't had the lovely Festus, Alana would have made a fantastic Finance manager at Righteous Anger, except no way could they have afforded her. Sweeping into the agency as a supervising auditor when Isabel had discovered major malpractice three years before, and scaring them all to death, she now supported them by virtually subsidizing Steph's salary so she could even live in London at all, and also sent regular tranches of money in Caroline's direction which Steph didn't even know about.

Bel covered her own costs by extensive consultancy work, and Caroline managed to get enough grant funding to work their projects, cover the core costs of a London office and pay for Trixie's salary. Otherwise they would be all working out of a garden shed somewhere west of Reading with cocoa tins for telephones.

Anger these days, righteous or otherwise, just wasn't very profitable. Generous people liked to sponsor children or put in water pumps. Fighting battles and raging against governments had never been nearly as popular as tear-stained babies, and anything political or structural was currently deeply threatening to the newly elected government, blown in by a populist backlash against boring experts and the European insistence on co-operation rather than competition.

Steph watched Alana snip and fold, and tape, and hoped their love-making the night before had healed some of her lonely sore places. She still had the feeling, though that Alana had a great head of emotional water dammed up behind that cool exterior, and that very soon it might come flooding over the top.

She had things she wanted to share too, but she was frightened for them both. Could they manage those sorts of conversations and not hurt each other? Where even to begin? It was difficult, and Christmas coming on top with the added tension, and expectations of peace on earth and joy to all, made it so much harder.

"I'm going to put a load of laundry on. I still haven't unpacked entirely from Kinshasa."

"You should, but don't leave the washing wet in the machine like I've known you do before. It will all go musty."

"We have just enough time for me to hang it all up on the radiators, don't worry."

"Let's leave at 1 pm then. The Mazda could do with a run. All the trains will be over-booked up to Sheffield anyway."

Alana's little car was parked at the back of their flat. She rarely used it in London but didn't want to give it up altogether. It was rather a silly car, a two-seater sports model, a Mazda MX5, what one of her brothers had dismissed as a "hairdresser's car."

But she loved it. It was a shining sapphire blue, and when you put your foot down, it felt as if you were going eighty, when in fact you were only going fifty. It looked racy but was in truth a secretly well-behaved car for a well-behaved woman.

While Steph waited for her washing to dry she thought she'd do some more research into how and where they might find out about her mystery girl. Googling "trafficking" pulled her away from Africa into news from far nearer to home though. She read article after article with increasing interest.

The Parliamentary committee on sex-work in the UK had recently published a report which spoke about sexual exploitation of young women on an "industrial scale", and made many recommendations, none of which as far as she could see had been implemented.

Then she clicked on the name of the committee chairman and saw he was a Labour MP who had just lost his seat in the previous week's election. Disaster then for what his committee had probably hoped to do! All the parliamentary committees would have been disbanded by this General Election, and it would probably be many weeks before they would be reconfigured.

Stephanie began to think hard. She was a born campaigner and writer. She loved getting her teeth into a national scandal, like a Yorkshire terrier and shaking it until it dropped all its secrets.

For the next few weeks, she was going to take her frustration over all the young African girls she had seen pushed into sex-work, and her worries over the young person on the plane, and channel them into some active work on what was happening under her nose here in the UK. London was full of sex-workers, and she wondered who was profiting most from their labour.

Steph's plan also still tied in with Isabel losing Carrie, her previous partner, to violence over much the same thing, trying to expose trafficking gangs from Eastern Europe. Isabel had never been given closure over that, and surely she owed it to her boss to dig out more of the facts.

If she could track the routes by which girls came into the UK, and the gangs of traffickers who exploited them, then it would be the best use of her time before the next overseas posting was necessary. She knew Alana wanted her to stay home for at least a month or so anyway. As had happened so often before, Steph could sense a new crusading obsession coming into her mind, and it felt good.

"How are your Christmas parcels coming on, darling?" she asked. "The washing's done, so we can be away in an hour at the latest. And can I drive? You'll go far too steadily if we are to get to Mother's before dark."

Alana had finished wrapping the presents and had arranged them in two neat piles, one small, for Stephanie's family, and one larger for her own tribe.

She said, "Here, sit down over here and write the tags. Do you remember yours by shape, or do you need me to remind you what they are?"

"You'd better remind me. Mum will be given a set of drill-bits otherwise. That won't look good on my daughterly record."

"Your mum's OK. She's just lonely. Did you know she used to call me every week while you were away, just to get some more news and an update on how you were?"

"Oh, Ally, I didn't know. You never said."

"I was happy to do it. We both liked talking about you. We both love you very much, you know."

Steph felt the unspoken reproach sink like a stone down between them. Her mum had even bought herself an IPad so she could get skypes from Steph, and she knew she had initiated those calls far too infrequently.

She felt like a selfish bitch. Alana passed her a pen and she sat at the table and wrote loving messages on all the tags Alana had attached. The weight of things unspoken had invaded their flat again, and she knew it would be here to stay until she allowed Alana the space to open up.

But Alana changed the subject rather abruptly.

"One thing I think we should do before we lock up and leave, is phone Montreal. It's our last clue, and by the time it's 1 pm here, it will be 8 am there. Let's wait until we've packed up, but call then. We'll know after that whether we need to chase up Russians anymore."

"Yes, good idea. Though I would like to contact Phil Cooper anyway. He's worth knowing. You'd like him."

And Alana nodded in agreement. Steph noticed she'd managed to save half a metre of the expensive coloured paper and watched her in admiration as she folded it up and put it away in the drawer. Nothing Alana touched ever was left casually around. She never, ever, tolerated a loose end, and Steph was only too aware that her whole life, apart from

Alana's section of it, was just a whole jumble of loose ends.

"Your washing's finished. I can hear the washing machine singing that tune it makes to tell you when the cycle's finished," she was reminded.

"I'm on it. By the way, you look very sexy in that dressing gown. Shall we just go back to bed for the weekend and forget about driving up North?"

"No. Not after I've worked so hard. Now go!"

And Steph went, festooning all the radiators throughout the flat with her clothes, which because they were all ergonomically and scientifically designed for global explorers, would dry pretty speedily in the warm air.

At 1 pm, they called the Canadian number. It would be 8 am in Eastern Canada, a completely civilised time to call on a Saturday morning. This was the only number apart from the Congo Brazzaville number which worked with just the addition of a country code.

Steph listened as the call went through and then the reassuring regular beep of a number successfully ringing. It rang several times, but then, just as her hopes were beginning to fail, the phone was answered, in French, by a neutral sounding woman's voice.

"Bonjour, La Convent of Notre Dame Maria Immaculata."

Stephanie took a mental leap sideways and then back, rather like a knight in a chess-board beating a hasty retreat. It was not the answer she's expected. But her agile brain managed to adjust and she asked to speak to someone in authority if possible. The woman must have heard her English accent, and answered her in English, well Canadian English anyway.

"I am sorry. All the sisters are on retreat until Christmas Day. No-one is available. Please call back on December 26th or later. If you would like to book a retreat for the New Year, our office will re-open then."

"No, I'm sorry, but I am trying to follow up on a request from a young West African woman I met on a flight, who wanted me to contact her sister. Do you have anyone there from West Africa by any chance? All I have is this phone number, but no names."

"We cannot give out any personal details of members of our community."

"Well, could I maybe email a request through, and if this resonates with any of the nuns, maybe they could email me back. I've been working in the Democratic Republic of Congo you see. I'm quite genuine. I'm concerned for the young woman."

The receptionist, or whatever she was, grudgingly agreed and Stephanie took down the email address and full name of the religious house.

"So if I send this off to you, it will be read on December 26th and someone might respond?"

"C'est vrai. That's correct."

"Well, thanks."

"No problem. Goodbye."

Steph turned back to Alana, who was filling a thermos with hot black coffee for their journey.

"Don't you just hate it when people say "No problem", when they are making the problem?"

"Any luck though?"

"I don't expect so. They sound a very stuffy Catholic set up of female Religious, all of whom have gone into retreat until after Christmas. But I do have an email address to send to. You never know. There are quite a few North American Catholic missionaries still operating in DRC. The kid's sister may have joined them. Let's keep our fingers crossed."

"Google them anyway. I expect they'll have a website, and you can see if they have a centre of operations anywhere in West Africa."

Stephanie followed Alana's prompt and did indeed find a website for the convent. It seemed they ran schools in Canada, and yes, still in Francophone Africa. Stephanie instinctively rebelled against the missionary zeal of the colonial era expansionism into the Congo.

French and Belgian Catholic communities were still all over the country, but Steph's real anger was towards the 'holy roller' North American Pentecostals whose local branches and pastors had disastrously encouraged local communities to turn against their own children and brand them as witches. The torture and misery inflicted on innocent children as a result of this evil syncretism knew no bounds.

It was fed by the wretched poverty and corruption by the powerful which had spilled across the vast country ever since the earliest days of the Belgian invasions in the 19th century. The country's kids were just collateral damage. And the one girl she had met on the plane crystalized for her the issue. She would find her, she must, and somehow she would rescue her from what was frightening her.

Steph couldn't get the girl's terrified face out of her mind. Swallowing her prejudices and misgivings about emailing the Convent, she sat down and wrote a brief, quite formal message and clicked Send.

"Well, it looks like everything is on hold till next week. I've made the coffee. Let's go!" said Alana. And eventually, after they had grabbed a sandwich, that's what they did."

A Girl on the Plane

Chapter 7

Way Up North.

Travelling from the far southeast corner of London round to the M1 motorway to head up to the north of England was never going to be an easy drive, and on the last weekend before Christmas it was predictably hellish. Alana was a competent and accurate driver, but even her patience was exhausted by the time they made it up to the North Circular Road, and then crawled slowly on towards the motorway.

It was already 2.30 pm and the scant allowance of useful daylight was begin to disappear. It was the shortest day. Many cars had their headlamps on, and the lights bounced off the wet roads.

They had stuffed every available gap behind their seats with presents and their overnight cases were squashed into the tiny boot behind. Steph had up curled her long legs, so she could relax back in the passenger seat and admire Alana's profile to her right, but it was still a struggle to get comfortable.

"Maybe we've outgrown this car," she said, as they slowed down for the twentieth red light in the last three miles. "Or maybe I've been spoiled by all the giant four-by-four people-carriers in Africa."

"I guess you have," replied Alana. "I love my little Mazda, but you are right. It's not exactly a family car."

This seemed a possible way to start talking about the big thing she wanted to open up to Steph about. She had decided to go to what she really wanted, and not mention the American job offer, which would very much be a default position. They had four hours ahead of them to talk about it without interruption. She decided there would be no better opportunity, and took a deep breath. But Steph cut through and interrupted her train of thought.

"More than that, sweetie, it's not exactly green. Since Isabel's been writing her book on global warming, she's getting hot herself about cutting carbon emissions and urging us all to think green as much as we can. I know we're in for an environmental audit when she gets back to work in January."

Alana said, "The electric cars are still very expensive, and the only trips we make by car are all long ones, so we would need to recharge at least once. But you're not wrong. I'm going to start researching them. Maybe we can lease an electric vehicle."

OK, first little opening pass, skillfully deflected into the long grass, Alana thought. She'd try another shot.

"I had such a good time last night. You were lovely. It's been so long, I almost forgot how much I enjoy being having sex with you. It was a perfect start to Christmas. You know, you are very gifted at, you know, making love. You have a great natural talent in that area."

Stephanie laughed out loud and stared at her. Alana felt her cheeks going pink and realized she'd sounded like she was giving Steph a reference for a job as an escort or something.

"What brought that on?" Steph asked. "You do understand, don't you, that most of what I know about making you happy in bed, came straight from your own tutorials? Don't you remember, when we first met up and tried to start something, how hopeless I was, how astonished you were at my stupidity? I may have looked like I should know what I was doing, but I was embarrassingly awful at it. Go on, you must admit it. I was thirty going on thirteen. I almost didn't even know I was gay!"

"But you knew enough to fall in love with me. That was what mattered. That's the only thing that mattered to me. And I fell right back for you like a ton of bricks."

"Yeah, you did. I was so astonished and excited. I was like a kid in a candy shop."

Finally! Well, they were agreeing about something at any rate, and at last, they had made it onto the motorway. Alana could relax her navigational skills for the next four hours or so until they turned off for Sheffield, Steph's home town. She took some courage from Steph reminding her how she had had to manage their initial love affair from the start, and almost give her some elementary biology lessons. She was the senior partner after all. She had to go for it . . .

"Steph, now we are together again, thank God. I really need to talk. There's some big stuff I want to share, to discuss with you."

"Huh, what?"

"Steph, listen. You know I love you, to the moon and back. I always miss you dreadfully when you're away. And I want us to do it differently from now on. I need you to be home more. I need you with me. I do. And also..." Here she gulped and took a flying leap of faith. "... I think we're ready to move on to the next phase in our life together. I want us to have a baby together, to be a family, to be a proper family with a child. And I think you should be the one to have it. Our baby, I mean. I think it would work better that way."

There, she'd said it! Well, half of it at least. She'd shot the thunderbolt up into the sky and there was no retrieving it now. She looked across at Steph. But Steph had gone quite white with shock under her tan. She just stared at Alana, her mouth open.

Alana bit her lip nervously. "I bet you didn't expect me to say all that, did you? Only it's been in my head for months. Sorry if it all came out in a rush."

Steph looked as though she'd just swallowed a large fly.

She croaked, "But, but, well yes, you're right about that. I never expected anything so completely crazy to come out of your mouth. Alana, you're bonkers. Certifiably bonkers."

"Why do you say that? We're both well into our mid-thirties. I'll be forty in two years. We are serious about each other, aren't we?"

Steph looked as if Alana had just given her new information she'd never considered before, just as though a reminder of their ages was a bombshell out of the blue. Alana wondered if Steph had ever considered the need to change their dynamic at all. If she hadn't, didn't that say something rather worrying in itself?

Surely every couple would naturally move on, wanting to

deepen and mature their relationship, wouldn't they? It wasn't so outlandish to want to talk about the future.

Steph said nothing more for several long worrying seconds and then replied.

"Well, yes, of course, we're serious, I am serious. We're lovers. But what you've just thrown at me is in a whole new ball-game. You know my work is my life, my vocation, if you want to get heavy about it. I can't give it up. I just can't. Not for you, not for anybody. It's simply not possible. "

Alana's heart thudded down a few floors to the basement. She realized Steph wasn't even going to touch on her baby idea. Maybe that had been too much to include in the proposition straight away. But it lay at the very core of what she wanted for the future.

Three of her five siblings already had growing families, but it wasn't just wanting to keep up with them which had given her the idea. She knew she wanted to have her own children, to raise them, to have something, someone, on which to focus all her parental yearnings and hopes.

Her career in forensic accountancy, her ascent up the corporate ladder, all of that, well it kept her mind occupied, but her heart was completely unaffected. She was building her savings and a carefully chosen ethical investment portfolio, but she knew the main reason for doing it was to provide for Steph and their children in the future. She was already mentally nest-building in earnest.

But what to do, when her fellow love-bird simply wanted to fly off across the world, seeking new adventures all the time? Unlike the swallows, there wasn't even any regularity in Steph's comings and goings. She just constantly craved new adventures, new challenges. She was wearing her out, and sabotaging their relationship, didn't she see?

As soon as Alana had said, "I really need to talk," Steph's antennae had immediately vibrated with fear. She always remembered overhearing her dad saying to her mum, "Trudy, we really need to talk . . ." and then all the revelations came pouring out about his other partner, his other kids. Her ears started to ring as her blood pressure rose, and she had trouble even concentrating on what Alana was saying.

Her first responses had been from the gut, almost automatic, without thinking them through. Alana had been churning away on this inside her head for weeks, maybe even longer, but to spring it on her now, out of the blue, especially when there was no chance of escape, Stephanie couldn't stop herself feeling a white flame of pure anger at having been sucker-punched like that.

What Alana had said, and what she had heard, might not have been the same. She could only grasp that in effect Alana was pulling the plug on her whole career in development. That if they were going to stay together she would be grounded, imprisoned almost. She felt as though her stomach was rising up her throat, and that she was going to suffocate.

"And so, what are you saying? This is it? This is some sort of ultimatum? If I don't throw away my career, we're finished?"

"No, honey. But we have to talk, to find a compromise. I miss you so much when you're away, and it's getting as though you only drop in now and then to change your clothes and write your reports. Why don't you see that? Sometimes, when you're on the road, I don't even hear from you for weeks on end."

"Hey that was only once, and I was stuck three weeks in the back of beyond."

Steph felt a mixture of rising panic and now, inevitably some guilt. She couldn't defend herself. When she was working, often in extremely challenging physical and social situations, life back home, and the needs of Alana as her partner, often did fade into the background.

Clocking in even seemed like a chore sometimes, at the end of a long, hot, difficult day. But Alana had never travelled with her, never seen the hour- by-hour challenges, how could she understand a world she'd never had to encounter?

To deflect from the intensity of this sudden conversation, and to stop herself flying into a childish rage, which wasn't what she wanted to do, and which Alana certainly didn't need to see, Steph reached behind and pulled over the thermos of drink they'd prepared. She opened it carefully and poured out a few mouthfuls of hot, black coffee into the little cup, refastened the screw top on the flask, and took a swallow.

"Do you want some?" she asked her driver and passed the cup across.

Alana nodded and took the cup with one hand while she kept her eyes on the road. The little ritual helped them both re-balance, and then Steph tried to explain the strength of her response. The nonsense about a baby she wasn't even going to touch on at all. She concentrated on Alana's first big complaint about her being away too often and for too long.

"It's the nature of my job, having to work in the field, and yes, I know I get absorbed in the immediate issues, the day-to-day struggles. Life in a refugee camp, or a vast favela, chasing down ways to rescue kids from the criminal gangs or murderous police, fills my head when I'm there, whether it's in Asia, Africa, Europe, or Latin America.

"I am really sorry if I don't keep you in the loop some of the time, but you can't fully understand how intense things get. There is some danger a lot of the time, but also progress I can see happening. It gives me such a buzz when we get it right, when our partners achieve a massive win against the forces of darkness. Like the project we shared with partners in Bangladesh, getting kids out of factories and into school. They're making such good grades now. I need to schedule another visit there in the spring ..."

Alana snorted with frustration and Steph realized she had slipped back into her world without noticing. She listened as the inevitable complaining started again.

"That's so typical! You're addicted to your work to the exclusion of almost anything else. I don't think you've understood a word I've been saying. I spend long hours in my job as well, and it is important too, but I want a balance. I want a home life as well. I can't live the rest of my life like this, just providing you with some R and R after another tour of duty. It's worse than if you were in the army. Can't you see that? I'm hurting here. I've tried not to be selfish. I know your work is important. But you don't have to save the whole goddamned world single-handedly. You don't need a fricking Jesus complex to make a difference!"

Steph took a sharp intake of breath at this last salvo. Did

she have a Jesus complex? It was something her mother had alluded to once, in one of their frustrating and frankly depressing conversations about how absent Stephanie was all the time.

She was worried she was linking Ally and her mum too much in her mind, both people who wanted to limit her, pin her down. She had to see they weren't the same. They were completely different with different needs. Except she remembered Alana saying wistfully, "We often talk about you. We both love you very much, you know."

She thought for a few moments and then tried another tack. "Hey, look, when I next go off, like Bangladesh for example, why don't you come with me, take a few weeks' leave, come out and see the projects. That would be fun and we could be together all the time. I would love it if you did."

She could see the wheels inside Alana's brain suddenly start to spin into reverse as she thought about this hardly astonishing idea. Alana had never, in the three years they had lived together, even once asked if she could travel with Steph, yet it would make perfect sense.

Her boss, Bel, used to travel with her partner Carrie as often as she could. They had worked on joint projects, filming research, campaigning as often as possible, until Carrie's death, and Steph knew Bel had blamed herself bitterly at the time for not being there to protect and shield her in Eastern Europe, when she'd been shot dead by the sex-traffickers.

Maybe Steph could swing the argument away from it being her always in the wrong, to the constricting nature of Alana's office-bound existence. God, it must be so boring, chained to a desk all day, in a monochrome office, where the most exciting thing ever to happen was to discover a spreadsheet that didn't balance! She couldn't think of anything more tedious.

The afternoon was draining away with increasing miles under their engine. As they drove away from London, towards Northampton, Leicester, Nottingham, and finally up towards Sheffield, the darkness at the end of the year began to enfold them.

Alana said cautiously, "You know how I get very little

statutory leave, but I have a few weeks in hand for this past year I've not used. Maybe I might be able to come with you on your next trip. It doesn't mean my basic complaints aren't valid, and I still don't think you understand half of what I'm saying, but I'm not entirely ruling it out as an idea."

Stephanie drew what comfort she could from her girlfriend's cautious response, and decided they had done enough heavy furniture lifting for one session.

"Good, now let's not spoil Christmas anymore. You've got me here, now, in the flesh, and you know I think you are the sexiest woman on the planet. Let's make sure we have hot sex in every bed we sleep in over the holiday."

"Both our mothers will have a fit!"

"Nonsense. My mum's house has solid walls, and anyway she likes you more than she likes me most of the time. And I'm sure your mum and dad won't care either. I bet they still enjoy a healthy sex life."

"Stephanie! My parents . . . let's not even go there! The house will be bursting with family in every room."

"Then let's be thoughtful daughters and book into the nearest Premier Inn. I'm telling you girl, while I'm in the UK, sex with you is my absolute priority for the Christmas holiday, celebrating the birth of Baby Jesus or not. I'm sure he'd understand."

On that note, they were lovers and friends again, not antagonists. Alana turned off the motorway and headed for Stephanie's family home in the wealthy western suburbs of Sheffield.

Steph knew Ally loved it when she talked about how sexy she found her body. She breathed a small sigh of relief that their previous scary conversation could be buried under the up and coming holiday visits, hopefully pushed off the agenda by good food, present exchanges, and candlelight smooches on the sofa.

Her thoughts swung back to her mother's lingering depression. What Mum surely needed was a sex-life of her own. It was twenty years since Dad had left after all! She added finding her mother a suitable boyfriend to her list of forthcoming tasks, but remaining firmly at the top of the list was making Alana completely happy in bed and out of it, and wiping all the fantasies about Steph staying home and having babies out of her mind. God, what a nightmare that would be!

A Girl on the Plane

Chapter 8

"You choose your friends not your family."

They were both mightily relieved when Alana pulled up into the steep driveway and parked under the too tall trees which overshadowed the house. They stretched and began to crawl out of the low-slung Mazda. Steph's mother had lit the porch lamp and came straight through the front door into its pool of light when she heard the car arrive.

"My darling! Oh, it's wonderful to see you at last. Come here for a hug!"

Steph had an instinctive flinch, even as she embraced her mother for the first time in five months. Was the 'at last' intended as a reproach, or was she merely paranoid? Probably both. She remembered not having found the time for a late summer visit back to the family home before her trip to Kinshasa.

After listening to Alana's litany of complaints about her absence maybe she was just super sensitive. She loved her mum. It wasn't necessarily her fault if they lived two hundred miles apart, even when she was in the UK. She gave her a warm kiss now and a hug. Alana meanwhile was pulling their cases out of the car-boot.

Steph's mum ventured out into the sharply cold night air and helped her unpack, taking a case while Alana retrieved the first bag of presents from behind their seats.

"Hi Trudy, thanks. It is good to be here again."

They exchanged affectionate but not extravagantly matey kisses. From outraged disbelief, through tolerance and on to eventual grudging acceptance, Trudy's attitude to her daughter's girl-friend had certainly mellowed over the past three years.

By now, she and Alana were a team, a fan-club around Stephanie, who shared any snippets of information and updates they could glean about their loved one. Steph, who always assumed her brother was automatically the favourite sibling, never understood how important this was to them both, nor the mixture of love and exasperation she created in Trudy's heart.

Trudy's own mother had often quoted the old saying, *"A son is a son till he gets him a wife. A daughter's a daughter the whole of her life."* This would be true if her only daughter hadn't decided to run off to London, and then come out as a lesbian, and spent her working life mostly in places with unpronounceable names, campaigning on unwinnable issues!

On the other hand, Trudy could at least understand what Alana did for a living, and if she phoned her up, as she often did, on a Tuesday or a Sunday evening, she knew she'd find her at home, and open to a chat. It was little routines like that which kept her cheerful, or as cheerful as she'd ever be again, after the bastard Stephen had left.

TBS was her private shorthand for her ex-husband, after whom Stephanie had been named, and with whom she unfortunately shared her tawny athleticism, and hazel eyes. Looking at her, Trudy often saw her husband's ghost.

It was all she had left of him now. All they ever saw of him. She had a secret suspicion that Craig, her son, knew where he lived, and about the details of his secret second family, but the subject was never mentioned, and she had no desire whatsoever to open that can of worms. Stephanie had been her father's darling after all, and she had always loyally refused to have anything to do with him from the day he walked out. It was a rock on which Trudy could depend, and it shored up the stone wall of hatred she had built around her heart.

Now though, she was almost merry. She was determined not to spoil Steph's pre-Christmas visit by saying stupid things, or even worse, breaking down into shameful tears. She knew she had behaved badly on so many previous occasions. No wonder her daughter strictly limited her visits home.

"Come on in! I expect you are both starved. I've made a chicken lasagna, and there's a tiramisu for pudding. I know it's a favourite of yours."

"Yum-yum," said Steph, happy to oblige with matching enthusiasm. "Are we in my old room as usual, Mum? I'll just take the cases up, shall I?"

Having the absolute right to sleep with her girl-friend when they visited Sheffield had been a battle she'd fought in the first year of their relationship, and one she had thankfully won. An angry exchange of words had done the trick, and her refusal to be ashamed or compromise on the matter had actually worked. Her mother somehow understood this was a battle she wasn't going to win and caved in gracefully in the end.

"Yes, dear. I've turned up the radiator, and even switched on an electric blanket to air the bed. You come on into the kitchen with me, Alana, and let me fix you a drink. There's some mulled wine on the stove, and some nibbles."

Alana went through into a cinnamon-scented, large, and beautifully appointed kitchen. Steph's father had disappeared, but he had left his wife the large mortgage-free house in one of the leafiest and most prestigious areas in Sheffield. At the time of the divorce, both the children had been in their early teens, so it was only fair to let them all keep the family home.

Trudy rattled around in it on her own now much of the time, but she sometimes had Craig and family over to stay, and her work as a medical secretary gave her a daily outlet and a change of scene. She was rebuilding her shattered sense of self-worth, brick by precious brick.

Alana shrugged off her jacket and hung it on the back of the door. The homeliness of the kitchen, with the cheerful welcome she received from both Steph's mum, and the wagging tail of her elderly border collie, Meg, made her feel at home, and she sat down at the table and stretched both her arms above her head.

"It's good to be here," she said with an honest smile. The long drive, at the end of an exhausting week, and the difficult conversation with Steph, had all combined to make her yawn with tiredness.

Trudy pushed a bowl of little cheesy whatnots towards her. "Thank you for bringing my baby back home to me. At least we can still both stop worrying about her for a few weeks."

"Yes. But Steph's a tough cookie. Don't you think we worry too much? She's like a cat with nine lives. And she's asked me to go along with her on her next trip. Do you think that would work?"

Trudy seemed pleased to be asked for her opinion.

"I would feel easier if you were with her. You're so sensible Alana. Oh, I know she is too, normally, and experienced, but she was always reckless if she had a cause to fight. When she was only ten, she laid in hammer and fist at a gang of older boys she found tying fireworks to the tail of a kitten. She knocked the front teeth out of one of them."

"Wow! And she says she doesn't even like kittens!"

"Don't believe half of what Stephanie tells you, dear. I'd have thought you'd have cottoned on to that by now."

"Cottoned on to what?" asked the woman herself, coming into the kitchen and picking up on the tail-end of their conversation.

Alana smiled at her and passed the snacks across the table.

"Your Mum was telling me you used to like kittens as a youngster, and that you fought with older boys who were tormenting one."

Steph grabbed a handful of crisps and poured herself a large glass of the mulled wine from the jug her mother offered her.

"Any excuse to hit out at the male sex, I expect that was probably my motivation! Anyway, I was thinking, Ally. After supper tonight would you like to pop out with me for an hour, round to Phil Cooper's place? I've just called him and he's in. It's only fifteen minutes away by car. He could maybe try Moscow for us again."

Her mum though, cut her off at that point, with a tremor in her voice. "Stephanie darling, you've only just arrived. I need to see a bit of you for at least this evening! Please!"

Ally had raised her eyebrows as well, and Steph realized she'd put both feet in it again, getting her priorities all wrong, and forgetting her mother had been looking forward to this visit for months.

"Yes, of course. Forget it. I'm a thoughtless cow. And anyway, Moscow is way ahead of us timewise. Sometime tomorrow morning will do much better."

The other two had to be content with this half an about-turn, a compromise at least. And they moved forwards to eat the chicken lasagna supper which was bubbling so invitingly in the oven.

By being extra friendly and asking Trudy how her life was shaping up these days, showing a genuine interest in her girlfriend's mother, Alana managed to smooth over any more rough places and pinch-points in Steph's relationship with her mum, and the evening ended happily, as they watched a Christmas special re-run of the Graham Norton show on TV.

In fact, the visit so far was more relaxed than any Steph could remember from previous Christmases, when she had often needed to bolt out the door to go down the pub or just up on the moor, for a breather at all. She recognised her early suggestion of shooting out to see her old mate Phil, had been a reflex reaction in response to earlier, more emotionally fraught visits.

What they did all agree, before going up to bed, was that Trudy would accompany them out the following morning, to drop presents off with Steph's brother's family, then call on Phil and his wife, and then all go into Sheffield centre to look at the Christmas lights, and have tea in the winter gardens. That way, Trudy could feel included, not excluded. They would have Sunday night with her as well, before heading on to Manchester first thing on Monday morning.

Steph lay down in the double bed luxuriating in the warmth from the electric blanket beneath the bottom sheet, and watched Alana slowly strip. They were both wearing pyjamas, conventionally enough, but Stephanie's insides still tightened and her toes curled, as she watched Alana change from her day-time to night-time persona, saw her step daintily into the pale blue satin trousers, and pull on the oversized jacket. She had bought Alana those pyjamas, and chosen them especially large so there was plenty of wriggle room inside.

Alana removed the last of her make-up, brushed the hairspray out of her hair and took off her wristwatch and rings. Then she walked around the bed, and climbed in on Steph's right-hand side, straight into her open arms.

"It's the longest night of the year tonight," she mumbled, as Steph brought her closer, for an encompassing hug.

"Hmm, what a lovely thought," was the muffled reply, as their bodies fitted together like a pair of spoons. Then Step added, "'As snug as a bug in a rug', was what my Dad used to say when we were children and he tucked us in."

"Does coming home make you think of him?"

"How could it not? But I haven't seen him in twenty years. I don't even know if I'd recognize him."

"Of course you would. You know, if your mum could only find someone new, if she was happy, then maybe you might be able to ... "

"No, let's not even go there, darling. It won't happen."

"But, she's more relaxed tonight than she was last year."

"She's grown to love you. I can see that's one reason. She understands us better, and isn't jealous of you anymore."

"And was she at first?"

"Oh, of course! Don't you remember? How she could barely spit out your name the first year I brought you home?"

"Well, I think she trusts us now, that we'll stick together, that I will be here long term."

"And will you? Even after what you said in the car, about wanting someone to be there when you come in from work, that you want children, when clearly I couldn't ..."

Alana listened as Steph tried to step out over the thin ice again, and sighed.

"Yes, I'll probably be here. Have you not noticed, Stephanie Hunter, I am in love with you, damn it. I just hope we want the same things, that's all."

Steph heard the clock on a distant church strike eleven and knew the time for fruitless arguing was long past. She used her mouth for much more pleasant activities, and her last thought, as she switched off the electric blanket, was just how blazing hot her ice-queen lover was under the covers.

It was very late when they finally slept, and later again when they woke the next morning. Roll on Christmas! But at least their winter solstice had been celebrated in a very satisfactory way indeed.

A Girl on the Plane

Chapter 9

A girl with sad eyes.

Straight after breakfast the following morning, Steph called her old mate Phil and asked if it would be OK to call in just before lunch. He lived in the Netheredge area of the city, which wasn't too far from her mother's house, and close to the university.

"Do you want to stay for lunch? You'd be very welcome," he said, and Steph replied, "That would be great, as long as you can cope with three of us, my girlfriend, Alana will be with me, and my mum, Trudy."

"The more the merrier, Anna's mother Halina is here as well, from Ukraine, so your mum and she can talk to each other and compare hassled grandma notes!"

Steph yet again felt the universe was conspiring against her to make her feel some sort of nasty person who had denied her mother grandchildren, but at least her brother was filling the void.

"We'll try to be there by twelve, Thanks so much!"

They gathered up the gifts they had bought the day before for Steph's brother and sister-in-law, and niece and nephew. Craig and his wife Joanne had a lad of four and a little girl of two, and prompted by Alana who seemed well versed on age-appropriate toys for children, she had chosen accordingly.

Steph had bought little Toby a giant dinosaur making kit, complete with a little recording gismo which gave out a very realistic T-Rex roar, and Sylvie a beautiful rag-doll with hand-made knitted clothes. She knew there was no point in attempting a bit of gender-neutral promotion of anything mechanical to Sylvie, who showed no interest at all in her brother's collection of vehicles and tiny *Lego* superheroes. But she carried a doll round with her most of the time.

Trudy drove them in her Toyota Prius, and they arrived at Craig and Joanne's in time for coffee. The house, on a small housing complex in a Derbyshire village on the southern edge of Sheffield, was immaculate and pristine; it was hard to believe anyone under the age of fifty lived there, let alone under ten! Not a toy was in sight, nor even a child, but after letting them all in through the front door, Joanne went to the back of the house and brought forth her children.

"They were in their playroom," she said, explaining the lack of mess and toys in the main sitting room. But there were Christmas cards up on the mantel-piece and window sills, and a prettily dressed artificial tree stood in the corner. It all looked like a window display for a department store, and Steph, as usual, felt some sort of alien just landed from the planet Zog.

She didn't dislike Joanne and appreciated how happy she and Craig seemed to be, but she wondered how they had coped with the messy business of having any sex in the first place, let alone managed to procreate and have two children. Before they married, Joanne had worked for British Airways for seven years as an air-stewardess and retained all that attention to perfection in make-up and hair-style she been taught years before. If she handed you a biscuit, it always came with a neat little paper napkin. She had cream carpets throughout the house. She wore three inch heels all the time, even when she was home alone.

Craig, three years younger than Steph, had always been the one in their family to be tidy and organised, and he appeared soothed by Joanna's obsessive attention to details and hatred of clutter. He had gone into the world of financial management and now ran a successful brokerage, selling retirement packages and investment portfolios. Steph knew she wouldn't have lasted a week in such a boring environment, but she loved him anyway. Their father's absence from the time Craig had been ten, had brought them closer together throughout his teens.

They all sat down together on an L-shaped white leather sofa set, and Craig and Steph chatted, while Trudy went out into the kitchen to help Joanne bring in a tray of coffees. Alana, meanwhile, devoted herself to the children, who clustered round her and wanted to see what she had in her pockets.

Alana had picked up the trick from her Irish grandfather Seamus, and when visiting children always carried a little tube of sweets in her pocket, which she would produce as if by magic and pass round surreptitiously, as if they were a secret gift. She was a natural Mary Poppins. Toby and Sylvie, hardly remembering her from the last time she'd visited, still remembered the sweeties, and cuddled up close to her.

Coffee was passed, gifts were exchanged, and Alana's Japanese standard of gift wrapping was duly admired. She returned the compliment by saying,

"Joanne, your tree looks lovely. Beautifully done. Is it new? I remember last year you had purple and silver baubles."

"Yes, I've gone for Scandinavian this year. Red and white ribbons and some nice little gingerbread decorations I found in Coles in the centre of Sheffield."

Steph looked at the tree rather puzzled, and said, "I don't see any cookies."

Joanne wrinkled her nose, "Well of course not. That would encourage all sorts of mess and maybe even mice. No, these little ornaments are plastic of course, but they look real."

"Very charming dear," said Trudy, patting her hand. And Steph had yet another of her many unworthy thoughts, wondering if her mother preferred thc imitation lifestyle and ultra-hygienic mild affection of her daughter-in-law to her own messy but very genuine, pain-filled love. Mothers and daughters….why were their relationships so complicated?"

Joanne carried on describing all the preparations she'd made for Christmas. "I've decided on a turkey crown this year. Who needs all that messy carving of the legs, and what does one do with dark meat anyway?"

Steph couldn't help herself. "Where I've just been, they would run five miles for it. They even cook up the feet of any poultry they can get hold of, and the children suck on the bones."

Steph's words fell into a sort of chasm in the middle of the room, and her Mum looked embarrassed for her. It was almost as if she'd said a string of swear words or made a bad smell. Being constantly reminded of how wretched the rest of the world had it had long ceased to be fun for her family, she should have known by now.

Alana stepped in to smooth over the void. "Steph only landed two days ago. It's very hard, coming from the Congo, straight back in all the Christmas razzamatazz. But we had a great time Christmas shopping in Covent Garden market yesterday. The lights were lovely."

This gave them all something else to talk about, rather than hungry African children sucking on chicken feet, but Steph felt sad that no-one, not even Alana, had much clue what she'd lived through for the last three months. She felt lonely, even a miss-fit, and certainly not ready for the jolly-holly, jingle-jangle Christmas her country seemed to be wanting her to celebrate.

The story of Mary and Joseph, a penniless couple's struggle to find shelter to give birth, their tired donkey, the socially unacceptable shepherds, these were images far closer to her mood. If Christmas meant anything, it must been good news for the poor, not indigestion for the already over-indulged wealthy.

But she decided not to spoil things for anyone else. Alana had obviously guessed she was at the end of her tether, and stood up, giving the children a last round of hugs and kisses.

"It's been lovely, but we must push on now I think. We are going to visit Steph's old friend Phil Cooper to ask his advice about something."

They all moved towards the door, and then Craig said, "I remember Phil Cooper. Wasn't his elder brother your first steady boyfriend, Steph?"

Steph swallowed hard. It was something she hadn't hidden from Alana, her failed attempts at heterosexuality, but this certainly wasn't something she needed to have brought up again now. Alana hadn't even known what Andy Cooper's name had been, nor for how long they'd dated.

"Yes, like a lifetime ago. I'm surprised you remember."

"Oh wow, I remember you bringing them all home when you were at Bradford Uni. A whole string of fellows. But he was the best. He took me out on his motor-bike. What happened to Andy?"

"No idea," said Steph tightly. "I haven't seen him in fifteen years. Now we must fly. 'Bye everyone." And she almost ran down the drive, past the plastic reindeer grazing their electronic way across the front lawn.

Behind her she could hear Joanne saying brightly to her mother, "We'll see you 12.30 on Christmas Day then, Trudy, after we've had a chance to clear up the mess when the children open their presents."

She couldn't help but feel a pang of guilty sorrow for her mother, denied the spontaneous fun of being there to watch her captivating grandchildren unwrap their Christmas presents, and then no doubt sitting down to a carefully portioned and beautifully presented calorie-controlled Christmas lunch, all on Joanne's stylish porcelain plates and dishes.

Alana said nothing, as she sat in the front seat next to Trudy, who drove them back down the hill into Sheffield, and on to the district where Steph told them Phil and his Ukrainian wife lived. It was in a warren of steep terraced streets, and they had quite some struggle to find a place to park on the crowded streets.

Steph knew her lover too well though, and guessed a few choice remarks were being stored up ready for when they were alone. They all walked round the corner to where the Cooper family lived, and were admitted to a completely different environment to the one they'd just left.

The narrow passageway, full of little boots and jackets hung up on a peg opened up into the small but very cheerful front room, still with an open fire, and piles of presents and home-made decorations. Two children were sitting at the table drawing, while they were also watching children's TV. On the screen a giant black rabbit dressed in dungarees seemed to be keeping them occupied.

Steph guessed Phil was doing well, for a struggling academic. He had tenure in the social studies department at Sheffield University, which was an achievement in itself, and had also managed to put the deposit down on this three-storey terraced stone house just before the prices rocketed out of reach. Now he was very much a family man, with three kids in primary school, a wife, a dog and a huge mortgage. His editorship of the journal couldn't bring in much income, being much more a labour of love.

Not that it seemed to weigh him down too much.

"Stephanie! Fantastic to see you again. It's been far too long! Come and meet Anna and Halina."

"Hi, and this is my mum, Trudy, whom I don't think you'll have met, and my partner Alana, whom I know you haven't."

Phil warmly shook both their hands and ushered them through into the back room, which was only slightly less cluttered with children and their toys. The scrubbed pine table was set for lunch.

"Hope you don't mind soup. It's Halina's speciality."

Anna came forward and beckoned to them to sit down. "My mother always said, "When there is nothing else, there can always be soup! When I was a child, we lived on it.""

She was a tallish girl with slim bones and sad dark eyes. She kept looking across at Phil as though she worshipped him, which was nice. Steph asked, "So how did you two meet? Do tell."

"Later maybe," Phil replied. Was there a slight hesitation there? He continued, "First, tell me what you would like me to do. How can I help?"

Steph talked about the girl on the plane, and their problem working out whether the phone number they had could relate to any address in Eastern Europe, and whether he could call the number and make enquiries in Russia.

"My spoken Russian's pretty basic, but Anna will certainly try the number for you. That's no problem, but let's eat now, and you can tell us the full story over lunch."

Then he went out of the room to shout to his children to come in for lunch. They tumbled in and sat on the wooden benches around the table. Granny Halina, who bore all the hallmarks of a hard life, with her cheeks hollow from losing most of her teeth, and her face and hands weathered with swollen knuckles.

She was about the same age as Steph's mum, or within a year or so at the most, but they looked quite different. Trudy's clothes, her hairstyle with its subtle highlights, and her smooth and slightly scented skin, spoke of self-care and a generous budget. She may have had her heart broken but it wasn't at the expense of her bank balance.

The soup, from a mixture of root vegetables, red peppers, and potatoes was very tasty though, and they all enjoyed the meal and the eastern rye bread which accompanied it.

"Are you visiting for Christmas?" asked Trudy, to make conversation with Halina.

Anna translated, and then when her mother nodded, added for her, "My mum hopes to come live here with us when it is possible, but it is currently very difficult. Phil's income isn't sufficient to qualify to apply for more than a tourist visa, but we hope for the best. There is nothing now for her back in Ukraine."

"How did you come to the UK?" Steph asked Anna as she tried to pick up the trail which Phil had left rather cold.

"I came after job, but it didn't work out. I wanted to be dancer. I met Phil through agency which was working with people from Eastern Europe."

Anna had the same language trait many Russian speakers had of missing articles from in front of her nouns. Stephanie thought it was rather cute. Anna must have been in the UK for at least twelve years, for her eldest girl was eleven.

Phil then chipped in and said, "Why don't we all have some spiced Christmas tea, and Anna and her mum can talk to your mum in the other room while we look up this phone number. You need to tell me the story. "

Over drinks, Alana and Steph told him the full story of the girl on the plane, and how worried they were for her safety.

"African connections to Russia? It seems a very long shot."

"We know. It's mainly to eliminate the possibility. But we do know there's been a lot of trafficking activity in and out of Russia and Moldovia especially. My boss Bel Bridgford has done a lot of work on it. She lost her partner who was making a film when she was shot and killed three years ago."

"Carrie Montarini? I remember it well. In fact, I met them first when we were involved with a not dissimilar case, someone Anna had known from her home city in Ukraine who worked in one of those so-called massage parlours in London. I never realized that you work for Bel. She's one of the best campaigners I've ever met. What is she up to these days?"

"Climate Change. She's just finished a ground-breaking book about its effects on vulnerable communities across the world. But she was in a terrible car-smash last May and has only just recovered. Oh, and she's married her assistant, a young medic called Bryony."

"Wow! That's romantic!"

"Sure is! And it's a small world."

"Hmm, so show me the number. And what prefix did you use when you rang Russia?"

"Just the country code. They put the phone straight down as soon as we spoke though. All I managed to say was "Do you speak English.""

"Let's get Anna back in. If I speak, they will pick up the English accent immediately and we may get off to the wrong start."

So they called Anna back and left the two mothers sitting together in amiable silence, while the children squabbled and chatted around them.

Anna quickly grasped what they needed, and she picked up the phone and punched in the long row of numbers. Then she embarked on a long conversation in Russian, peppered with several '*Dah*s', '*Niets*' and '*Spasibas*." It went on for some time, and the others were getting quite hopeful before she ended the call and shook her head.

"No good," she said, "unless your friend's sister is electrical installer in Vladivostok. They have never heard of any African girls. But we had nice exchange of views on the best way to cook dumplings. By the way, they said they would like to move to England, if we can arrange it, and can we send them IPhones."

Phil pulled a wry face. "You did say you wanted to eliminate the red herrings."

Steph nodded, a little wearily though, and Alana put the phone number paper carefully back inside her wallet.

Anna said, "Red herrings? How's that? Why are they red and why are we talking about fish here?"

"Just an English expression," explained Alana. "It means something like a wild goose chase."

"Gooses? Why do you chase them? Sometimes I think I will never get completely fluent in English. It is a crazy language!"

And they all laughed.

They were preparing to leave, when Phil pointed to a photo on their fridge of two sun-tanned guys in dark glasses, with their arms round each other's shoulders, standing on a mountain somewhere.

"Remember who this is?" he asked Steph. "Have you brought Alana up to speed with your misguided youth yet?" He turned to Alana and said, "It was through my brother that Stephanie and I first met. They were one big item all through their first year at Uni."

"Oh, is that your brother?" asked Alana, rather too chirpily for Steph's peace of mind. "He looks rather good, although it's hard to tell with the dark glasses."

"Yes, that's Andy, with his mate Ben. Ben works at the BBC now. He's an editor on the morning news desk and is based up in Manchester."

"What about Andy?" Alana obviously wasn't going to let this drop.

"Andy works for Oxfam. Country programme advisor for Afghanistan. I'm surprised your paths haven't crossed, Steph. I'll remember you to him when I next email him. He'd probably like to hear from you."

"I doubt it," said Steph quickly. "I dumped him, don't you remember? It was all very messy and painful."

"Well, I'll tell him you've switched teams. It will probably make him feel better."

"No, please, best just drop the whole idea. I don't want him to remember me at all. I'd quite forgotten him and it's a long time ago."

For once, her mother, who was listening to this exchange as she hovered in the corridor, stepped in very sensibly and said, "So it was. Thank you very much for lunch, Phil and Anna, but we must be getting on. I'm taking Alana and Steph down to the centre for a look at the Christmas display and to listen to the choirs singing carols outside the Cathedral."

So they left and re-emerged out into the wintry afternoon. Alana had slipped into the front room on her way out of the house and produced from her bag some little chocolate bears for the children who fell on them with delight. She'd made even more new friends, and they hung on to her and asked her if she could stay longer.

As they returned to the car, Steph said, "Well that closes off all our possible leads apart from the chilly sounding convent near Montreal, and I'm sure that will be a waste of time as well. It looks like we'll just have to give it up."

"Maybe for now, but let's see what happens after Christmas." Alana slipped her arms through Steph's and gave her a big kiss on the cheek. "Let's just enjoy the season for now. I've decided I like Christmas in Sheffield. Let's go down and listen to the carols!"

So that's what they did.

Chapter 10

Mean streets.

The mid-winter night drew in by four pm, and it was already dark when the three of them returned home to Trudy's warm and welcoming four–bedroomed house. Alana was just about to take off her boots and snuggle down for a quiet, comfortable evening, enjoying Steph's mother's home cooking, and the comforts of an open fire, when Steph's phone rang, and their programme then altered somewhat.

"It was Phil again," she said, sitting down next to Alana on the sofa. "He says he's been thinking about our quest, and there in someone in Sheffield, he's very keen we should meet. He said it's urgent."

"But we are expected in Manchester for lunch tomorrow with my parents. We won't have time surely."

"No, but he suggests we go back into town this evening, in fact, the later the better. His contact, Sheila Mitchell, runs a support group for prostitutes in the city, and she has links with people in Europe who are tracking the traffickers. He's given me her number and says it's a great opportunity to get some first-hand information about the sex-trade in girls, not just Europeans, but also from Africa."

Alana processed this quickly through her brain, and also noticed the slightly febrile nature of Steph's energy. It was obvious, that subconsciously she didn't want to spend a second evening with her mother, being reminded of her father's absence all over the house, and combating all sorts of mixed emotions about happy families.

Alana frankly didn't fancy turning out again into the dark, and sub-zero streets of Sheffield, however worthy the cause. She also felt sorry for Trudy, if they were going to abandon her for the evening.

"It's a good idea, Steph, but why not call this woman first and see if she's available, and if she is, why not invite her round to meet with us here? I'm sure your mum won't mind, and we don't want to leave her alone here. We're only here for two nights, after all."

"Why are you always so annoyingly sensible?" sighed Stephanie. "I was quite excited at the thought of running off into the night, interviewing women working the streets up by the Carfax. It's far more dynamic and interesting than watching something incredibly boring on the TV while eating our way through Mum's boxes of Quality Street."

"We don't do enough boring stuff. Sometimes it's good," replied Alana, unwrapping a purple chocolate wrapper as she spoke. "Well, all right. Make the call, and then we'll talk to your mum and decide together based on what you find out. But do ask her up here, this Sheila person, ask her here first."

The result of this conversation was that at nine p.m., with ample time beforehand for Trudy's beef and beer casserole to be served, eaten and digested, the front doorbell rang, and Steph went to answer it. The woman who came in seemed slightly surprised to see her and Alana, and a little overwhelmed by the warmth and comfort of their surroundings. She introduced herself and they did the same,

"Hi Sheila, we're so pleased you could come. Why don't we pop into the dining room and sit around the table to have a talk? Would you like a coffee or tea?"

"I'll take a mug of tea, thanks. I'm perished with cold! I can't stop for long, but I've left some of my volunteers in the bus."

"The bus?" Alana came forward and ushered her into the room. With hot tea at hand, they all sat round the table, while Trudy settled in for the Final of "Dancing on Ice" next door.

"Yes, we have a mini-bus, kitted out like a van, where we serve free hot drinks, and snacks and have a range of donated toiletries and supplies. We park in various places across the city centre, where the girls are working the streets. It's only on the weekend, Friday, Saturday and Sunday nights, but it gives them somewhere to rest and warm-up. The streets are mean for women like them."

Sheila was a woman in her sixties, northern, no-nonsense looking, dressed in jeans and a padded black jacket. Her hair was grey and long, tied back off her face, and she was bundled up with layers of sweaters and scarves, which she began to unwind.

She looked at both the younger women, and said, "So, I got your message and it intrigued me. But how can I help?"

Alana let Steph do the talking. "Essentially, we are worried about a young girl from West Africa, probably Congolese, who I met on a flight from Kinshasa to Brussels last Thursday. We think she may be in danger, and she gave me a phone number, saying she wanted to get word to her sister. But so far we can't trace the number, and with Christmas only three days away, we are exploring any leads we can. Phil said we should talk to you."

"Yes, so I understand. But who are you? Phil said you worked with Bel Bridgford." Sheila seemed to know the name well.

"Yes, I do. Do you know her? We work for the same agency in London. I'm the African Programme manager there."

"Righteous Anger?" Yes, then I know what you do, and I know Bel. I was one of her tutors at university twenty years ago. She's a remarkable person, who used to streak like a comet across the sky, but her girlfriend's death really knocked her back, devastated her, and wasn't she nearly killed in a road accident earlier this year?"

It seemed all the world knew and adored Bel Bridgford. Alana hoped Steph wouldn't take it the wrong way, because she'd achieved a great deal herself in making the world a slightly better place. But she needn't have worried. Steph had always worshipped Isabel, and simply took pride in hearing her praised.

"Yes, but she's recovered now, and has married. A young female student doctor. The wedding was arranged so quickly I couldn't get back to London for it, but Alana here attended for me."

Alana thought they should get back on track, especially if

Sheila's time was precious. "Please tell us anything you know which might help us track down the girl on the plane, or learn more about the dangers she faces."

Sheila was happy to oblige. "Oh, there's no doubt in my mind, from what you've told me, that your girl is definitely vulnerable to being trafficked. Gangs are waiting all across the world, but especially in and out of Western Europe on the look-out for fresh meat. And it is a meat trade, make no mistake.

"The women I work with are survivors of some very dark, violent situations. They may be adults now, working to support themselves and their kids, but many of them started in sex-work as young teens, managed and manipulated by criminal gangs who don't hesitate to get them hooked onto heroin or cocaine, are savagely violent towards them if they don't comply, and have no hesitation in making them conveniently 'disappear' if things get awkward."

"And would you say this applies to the majority of sex-workers in the UK?"

"No, not all, but it's a world-wide problem. Maybe not child-sex so much over here, though it depends how you define 'childhood', but for young vulnerable females, certainly.

"One route we have been looking into recently is the ferry route from Zeebrugge to Hull, which mainly carries freight. The big trucks are one way to bring in girls for cities across the UK. We're investigating this right now. And I do have one or two girls who use our services here in Sheffield, who are from French speaking West African countries, so many others must end up in British massage parlours and brothels. "

Alana wondered how much money was involved and asked about it.

"Tens of millions, when you take the whole trade. The girls at the bottom, who are sent out to work the streets, it's usually '£50 for a suck and a fuck.', but for the private clubs in London, Manchester, Glasgow, you can multiply that by 10 or 20 times. Of course, the women see very little of that money. Selling sex in our country is a highly profitable industry. Across the world, it is endemic, and the poorer the girls the worse they suffer."

Sheila swallowed her mug of tea and looked both angry and exhausted.

Steph asked her, "So how did you start your group? And how are you funded?"

"Probably like you, we started from a core group of a few women. I was a social worker, and I recruited a few enthusiasts. We have some grant funding, but public finance is hard to get, - people don't see street-girls and sex-workers as a worthy cause for coffee-mornings or flag-days. But some good churches support our work, and we have a couple of corporate donors, one of which gave us our mini-bus. Phil got involved, and that was how he met Anna."

"Anna? What do you mean?"

"Didn't they tell you?"

"No."

"Well then, Phil and Anna should be the ones to tell you. I am not going to break any confidence here."

Stephanie and Ally couldn't resist sharing a raised eyebrow glance at each other. What was Sheila saying here? Had Anna herself been a victim of trafficking. But it wasn't their business. Alana took them back to the task in hand and asked,

"Is there anything specific you can tell us which might help this particular girl?"

Sheila pulled out her notebook.

"Look, I can give you contact details in Belgium for a good group very similar to my own. They are called "Sœurs de la férocité, or Sisters of Ferocity, and are working with the Belgian police and have access to information, names of contacts in the Brussels area. It's not much, but it may help you. Though, without even knowing her name, I don't hold out much hope for you tracking down your girl on the plane."

Alana took down all the names and numbers Sheila dictated, and thanked her profusely for coming.

"Not a problem. It makes a change to come into a warm, middle-class home like this, and see how the other half live, even for an hour. Here's my card, by the way. Donations to our work are always welcome, and you can learn much more from the website. Let me know how you get on."

"We certainly will," said Steph, "and we appreciate your help very much. Here, please take £50 quid tonight for your trouble. Just buy a few more packs of tea-bags, or some fuel for your bus."

"Thanks," said Sheila, cheering up slightly at the couple of twenty-pound notes, and a tenner. "I won't refuse. Every little bit helps. If I was like Bel, I would have whipped out a bank standing order form and thrust it in front of you. But thanks anyway, and Happy Christmas."

They waved her off and closed the door. Trudy came out from the sitting room and said, "Another friend of yours? You see, there are lots of work you could do up here in Sheffield, if you want to change the world. You don't have to dash off to Africa to find people in need."

This was true, but Alana could tell Stephanie prickled a bit under the subtle criticism of her global perspective. The old biblical misquote of 'Charity begins at home' was so often used against social reformers who took an international perspective, and it was painful to Steph that her own mother bought into it.

But Alana knew the remark hid a great deal of anxiety and pain in Trudy about Steph's safety when she constantly flew into conflict zones. And if she was completely honest, she shared the same sentiment. It was getting late, and they all retired to bed.

Chapter 11

"It took me a while, that's all."

If Steph thought the piece of information Craig and Phil had both slipped out about her dating his brother had disappeared from Alana's brain, she was sadly mistaken. As she lay in bed, waiting for Steph to finish in the bathroom, she brought up the subject without even waiting for a suitable opening.

"So this thing you had going with Andy Cooper? Why have I never heard about it?"

"Nothing to say," mumbled Steph through the buzz of her toothbrush. Then she spat out and rinsed the basin. She came back into the bedroom, drying her hands on a small towel and looked quizzically over at Alana, who looked rather like a sexy barrister, propped up against the pillow with her reading glasses perched on the end of her nose, and a notebook and pen in her hands.

"Nothing?" Alana echoed, drily.

"Well, maybe something fifteen years ago, but nothing now. I haven't seen the guy since we graduated, for God's sake. And I split up with him when we finished the first year, two years previously. Poor Andy was just another casualty along my erratic journey towards coming out and realising I was never going to want sex with guys again."

"But you never told him about your confusion at the time?"

"Alana, I hadn't even told myself that in 2005, let alone anyone else. I just thought I was frigid and couldn't climax."

"But he must have meant something to you. Phil said you dated all through your first year at college."

"Of course he meant something. I was fond of him, but not like this, nothing like us."

"Did you sleep with him?"

"Yes. Naturally. Didn't you date guys when you were eighteen or nineteen?"

Alana looked rather shocked. "No I never did, not to sleep with them. I knew I was gay by the time I started my periods."

Steph pulled on her pyjamas and climbed up into bed next to her. "Well, that's good for you! You were lucky to be so sorted. I spent seven years in the wilderness trying to push my square peg into the world's round holes."

"So Andy Cooper wasn't the only one?"

"No, but why bring it all up again now? I have told you in the past that I used to date guys. Crikey, you virtually had to show me what to do when we first went to bed, don't you remember? I was a complete novice. You taught me nearly all I know. . ."

Steph had always felt a bit of a fool next to Alana, who had swept into her life and when she'd eventually been caught, lifted her previous fumbling attempts to be a lesbian into a whole new league of sexual excitement.

But she wasn't so inexperienced now. She fluttered her eyelashes with a deliberate flirty smirk, and leaned over Alana, removing her glasses, and taking her notebook and pen out of her hands.

"What the heck does it matter what or who I did all those years ago. I never cross-question you about your no doubt many lovers. I just want you now, here, and for evermore."

Then she kissed Alana's pretty mouth and put her hand under the jacket of her pyjamas. Alana cuddled against her and sighed rather wistfully. "I sometimes wish you did ask more questions, that you were just the smallest bit jealous. Do you not care about my exes?"

Steph hugged her with a real squeeze and chuckled. She now had enough sexual self-confidence not to worry about all those previous women with good taste who had bedded her girlfriend. But if Alana wanted her to be jealous, then she could put on a good show.

"Of course I care. But remember, I got the girl, not them. We've been together three years, and I want us to be together thirty years."

"Do you? Do you really see a future for us? In the long-term? We're so different, aren't we? Everyone makes a point of commenting on that, even our friends. I worry that I'm not exciting enough for you, that you feel trapped."

"Trapped? Never." Steph couldn't help mentally crossing her fingers as she said that. But it wasn't Alana who she felt was trapping her. It was the whole "settling down" idea. Maybe she was that thing which all girls hated in men, a commitment phobe.

But with her hand on her heart she could say she hadn't strayed once since she and Ally had become a couple, not that there hadn't been plenty of offers, in all the bars in all the places in the back of beyond where she had travelled. She might be neglectful, but she had never been unfaithful, and she had always come home.

"You know that you are the world to me, and you know I'd never cheat on you. I love you, beautiful bossy-boots

Then show me," whispered Alana. "I need a lot of reassurance right now."

Stephanie looked at her in the shadowy light from the lamp beside the bed and decided to be very reassuring. She pushed back the bed covers and eased herself up on the pillows.

"Well firstly, we can both take off these ridiculous pyjamas. Get out of bed and strip off now. I know you'll want to fold yours up and put them neatly on the chair. I'm just going to take mine off here and throw them into the corner!"

It was an opening salvo in what might become quite a stormy night, Steph wasn't sure yet, but she knew Alana liked games, liked to be bullied occasionally, just a little. Alana obeyed her, pretending to groan, but she left the bed, and did slip out of her pyjamas, and fold them up as predicted on the chair.

Watching Alana remove the offending pajamas, stand right before her naked and then move forward to join her in their shared bed gave Steph a delicious shiver of anticipation.

Alana's matching shiver wasn't only from arousal though. It was late December after all.

"Can I come back into bed now?"

Steph just stared at her, then rolled over and rested her head on one arm.

"Maybe"

"Please."

"Oh very well."

"At last! I might get frostbite out here. Stop tormenting me"

"You know I only do it to tease you. And you like to be teased."

"Hmm. No-one else is allowed to tease me. So why do I let you?"

"Because you know it's good for you. It's like mental tickling, and if it makes you laugh, your lovely eyes are like stars in the night sky. "

Alana came closer to the side of the bed, and simply stood there, slim, pale, and perfect.

Alana was as beautiful as a statue by Canova. Her eyes were dark violet-blue tonight, and her bone structure was up-lit by the bedside lamp so it shone like white marble.

She bit her lip in an unconscious hesitation or a fleeting lack of confidence, but her teeth were like perfect pearls, and her naked breasts spoke their own words of love as they stiffened with arousal.

"Come on, Steph. It's fricking cold out here. Let me into bed."

"You… are…so…lovely," whispered Steph, ignoring her complaint. "What have I done to deserve you loving me?"

She had herself been lying naked on the sheet. But she now rose to her knees and knelt up on the edge of the bed so she could wrap her arms around her woman. The heat already between them rose a few degrees. Steph could feel Ally's spine shiver under her fingers, and how the fine hairs at the top of her neck rose by a millimetre or two in response to her caress.

Alana now took Steph's head in her hands, and with a tiny groan bent her face, to give feather soft kisses across her forehead, her cheeks and her chin, before connecting with her mouth.

At that moment Steph knew she owned Ally, body and soul, and in return was owned by her. But Ally needed continual reassurance, and mouth to mouth resuscitation would put the energy back into her body.

Steph's hands slid south and cupped Alana's buttocks. Alana pushed and toppled her back over so that she fell against the pillows. They landed together with a thump, and Ally laughed, that sweet, low laugh she could produce when she was truly relaxed, and knew she was on her way to getting what she wanted, turning Steph into a frenzy of sexual energy, which in turn would enflame her own core until it exploded into multiple magnificent orgasms.

They rolled together on the bed, and Stephanie pulled up the duvet above them both.

"Put off the lamp, love," Ally told Steph, who could more easily reach the switch. "When I'm with you in the darkness, I feel we could be anywhere in the universe, just us, floating free, like spirits."

Stephanie obediently reached up and over and flicked the switch. Then she said, "But I don't want to be just a spirit. If that was true then I'd so miss your beautiful physicality. You make love to all my senses, I adore to look at you, to feel you, to smell you, to hear you."

She wrapped her arms round Ally, and smoothed her hair.

Ally whispered, "You missed out 'taste'. The taste of you is what turns me on more than anything else"

She managed to continue, "You're right though. I don't want to be a spirit just yet, even though sometimes I feel my body isn't as young and as flexible as it was."

"Sshh. don't start on that, or I will tie you to the bedpost and force you to wait while I kiss every inch of your body before I let you come."

"There aren't any bedposts on this bed."

"Hmm, you're right."

"Maybe back at the flat, we could treat ourselves to a few toys, jazz things up a bit?"

"I can have more than enough fun just with your wonderful body.

"There you go. You're worse than me."

Now, in these lovely hours towards midnight, it was just

the two of them, and they could play and pleasure each other as much as they liked. This was what Alana missed so much, what she had yearned for over the past lonely months. She'd had to fantasize and day-dream far too much.

But this midnight hour Steph's own mind was fully in the present, and she had no interest in day-dreaming. Her current activity was so delicious it left no room for external thoughts.

She was dropping kisses like red hot lava all along Alana's collar bone, while already invading her secret places with her hand. She now had her where she wanted, and moved down to kiss each breast very sweetly, almost demurely. But Alana bucked under her wicked right hand and knew what was coming. Her nipples tightened into hard buds, and she began to pant.

Using her own hands and mouth, Steph concentrated on making Ally want to scream, as she nibbled her collar bone and then kissed her ear until she could hardly stand the tickling. Alana had her arms tightly wrapped around Steph's upper back, stopping the descent of that wicked mouth, but eventually was forced to relent. Steph's need was simply too strong. Ally relinquished her hold and stopped her attempts at kissing. She just lay back.

Steph licked her way into Alana, and tasted the overflowing liquid bubbling unbidden from inside her. It was like ambrosia, and the more excited Alana became, the wetter was the whole experience, which Stephanie adored. There was no need to use her hand. Ally was coming against her tongue

Steph knew she could make it happen again. She raised her head and shifted up her body, so that her hand could take over. Then she plunged the middle three fingers on her right hand deep inside. Steph had explored every hill and vale of her sexual landscape, and knew just how to give the stimulation and rhythmic massage which brought a repeat climax within a few minutes.

Stephanie would have gone for the winning post of a third orgasm, but Alana surprised her by deciding to grab the reins and take control. She did this effectively by using her strength to flip Steph over, so she was now beneath her, and took her to her own climax far too fast and almost too roughly to be altogether comfortable. But it was how Steph liked it. Alana had understood this early on, and gave her lover what she wanted.

Their breasts lay against each other, one set pale as porcelain, the other golden with hot climate exposure and an easy tan. But in the dark, they were identical in their warmth, their beauty, and the arousal they gave to each other. Their breathing settled into its familiar pattern.

Stephanie kept Alana's small hand firmly between her legs and as she was finally falling asleep, her hand still possessively cupped between Alana's buttocks, she sent up a little prayer of thanks. At least Alana hadn't gone back to the weird idea of making a major lifestyle change and the idea of her having a baby. Maybe it had not been as big a deal as she'd thought it was, and she could relax. They could both relax. What a relief that would be.

Chapter 12

"I have my reasons."

On Monday morning, parting from Trudy with genuine hugs and kisses, and with her mother's presents for them both pushed down behind the seats, they started up the Mazda MX5 for the trip over to Salford, and began the next stage of their road-trip round the north of England. It was a grey December day, and the route from Sheffield across the Pennine hills, over the Snake Pass, was shrouded in low cloud and a heavy drizzle which blotted out all the distant views over the moors and woodland.

Alana was happy to let Stephanie drive this time, and she enjoyed the opportunity to get behind the wheel. The sports car rode low on the road but it had a good feel about it, the gears were tight and well positioned, so it had excellent acceleration and torque round the twisting road. Their route was a famous one for rally drivers, and even with the amount of pre-Christmas heavy freight traffic causing multiple slow-downs and delays, it was still a very pleasant run.

"I can't help feeling sorry for your mum, having to spend Christmas Day with Craig and Joanne. It will be so sterile and controlled, not much fun. It would have been better if we had stayed with her," said Alana, looking out at the wet fields and sodden cattle standing out in the rain.

"But we're off to see all your family. You wouldn't want to miss them out."

"No, but maybe next year we could do it the other way round, go to see them all first, and spend Christmas in Sheffield. That's unless we have a baby by then, of course, in which case…"

"Alana!" Stephanie nearly skidded the car in her need to

cut the conversation off at its knees. "No, I told you. That is a really stupid, stupid idea. Please don't bring it up again!"

"But why? Even after our lovely time last night? Why does even the possibility make you so angry? Can't we discuss it rationally? Just tell me your reasons. You owe me that, don't you?"

Steph summoned her inner Buddhist and tried to channel a sense of Zen- like calm to stop the crazy thumping of her heart.

She said nothing for another mile or two and then started to speak. "I do have my reasons. Well, there are many sensible reasons, but if you need me to lay it all out before you, the main reason is that I know I'd be a lousy parent."

"Why?"

"Because I'm not kind and caring like you. I'm basically selfish and self-centred. I never think to carry sweeties in my pocket in case I meet a child. I never want to nuzzle babies and kiss their little necks. Given the choice, I'd rather we had a dog, if I'm honest. Wouldn't a nice fluffy dog do it for you? I'll buy you one of those like a shot if you want one. Then you wouldn't be so lonely when I have to travel."

She waited for Alana to argue back, as of course, she did.

"I think you judge yourself far too harshly. Look how hard you drive yourself in the service of others. You never rest. What about all the African children you've helped to save, or the child workers in Nepal? You set up those whole campaigns. You've helped thousands of children, and their parents."

"Yes, but that's the point. I have always made sure someone else put them to bed at night and told them a bed-time story. I just don't think I'd be any good at mothering. Not everyone is, Alana. Just face it, it's probably just not for me."

Alana said nothing to that, just looked very sadly out of the car window again, and Stephanie felt a complete heel. She didn't like the silence between them, so she continued, trying to explain feelings, she hardly understood herself.

"Also, if you want the honest truth, I don't think I could cope with the physical side of it all, being pregnant, giving birth. It scares me just to think of it."

"Why? I expect you've seen many women give birth in your line of work, haven't you? Women in Asia and Africa?"

Steph nodded, and immediately had flashbacks to the sounds of screaming and moaning, of tiny babies dropped onto thin straw mats in the Philippines, of watching an infant born dead in Uganda, or women across the world pushed to a health clinic in a wheel-barrow, and dying in the delivery room in Ethiopia. Maybe she was a wimp about the whole process for some very good reasons.

But Steph's reluctance to think about babies had its roots even further back and they went very deep. Something which she and her mother never discussed, and which she had never shared with Alana, was her memory of the time when she was five years old and Craig was two, and her mother had fallen backward down the stairs, after her heel caught on the carpet.

Her mother had screamed as she fell, and then banged her head hard on the tiles in the hall. Stephanie and her little brother had both watched in horror as a great pool of sticky red blood began to spill out from under their mother's skirt and trickle across the floor.

Steph had never been so frightened, before or after, as she was that day. Her mother had moaned to her to fetch the phone and she remembered dragging it with its curly lead across the hall-way, the whole thing still attached to the wall.

"I'll dial 999", croaked her mother, as white as a sheet, "and when there is a voice the other end, I want you to say we need an ambulance. Explain what's happened. You need to be a brave girl for me and do this."

"But Mummy…"

Trudy, however, had then passed out, and she hadn't even had time to make the call. Steph had gingerly lifted the receiver and pushed her finger into the hole on the dial with 9 inside it. It was heavy for her small hand, but she managed, just about. Then she did it again, and again.

There was a funny noise, and then, like a miracle, someone grown-up the other end was talking to her. Little Stephanie had cried "My Mummy, my Mummy! She's fallen down the stairs and there's lots of blood."

The operator had quickly gathered she was talking to a five-year-old and just kept her talking. Where did she live, did she know? Which town, which street? Stephanie couldn't answer with anything factual, apart from the fact that they lived on a hill.

The operator then asked her if she knew the name of her primary school, which she did, and this must have helped identify the neighbourhood. They kept her on the line long enough to trace the call, and eventually a huge white ambulance had arrived outside and two men had carried her mother away on a stretcher. It was a night of terror and shock for both her and Craig, and the only thing she remembered the ambulance crew saying was. "Shame she lost the baby," as they shut the doors.

For some reason, Stephanie imagined they were talking about her, that she had lost the baby. Which baby? What baby? There wasn't a baby in the house. How could she have lost it?"

The para-medics had knocked on the neighbour's house next door, and she had presumably told them how to contact Steph's father, and taken the children in until he returned home. Stephen Hunter was never a hands-on father when they were small, but he must have managed somehow or probably her Granny had come over from Bakewell to look after them. But Steph remembered little of those days.

But when her mother finally returned home from hospital, she remembered some sort of bitter dispute going on between her parents, and her father saying at one point, "Trudy, it's for the best. We don't need any more bleeding kids round here."

So the baby had been bleeding? Was that why there was so much blood? Little Stephanie had been so traumatized by the whole episode, she never talked to her Mother again about it, in case she too, asked her where she'd lost the baby? And though, when she was old enough to understand all about miscarriages and concussion and knew none of it was her fault, she still had an instinctive fear and terror of losing babies, and of everything to do with childbirth.

Certainly, there had been no more babies in the Hunter household. And a deep groove of silence seemed to be cut down the middle of their family, between her father and mother, which grew deeper year by year. She never remembered them spontaneously laughing much together after that, and her Dad travelled away on business more and more frequently and for longer.

So this, Steph acknowledged, was why she was frightened by childbirth and all the physical risks involved, not only for herself, but also, maybe even more so, for Alana. At least Alana wasn't suggesting she be the one to get pregnant, thank God. But part of her wanted to know why not? It was Alana who was suddenly as broody as an old hen, after all.

Stephanie decided not to get psychological and talk to Alana about Trudy's lost baby, so she stepped back onto solid ground where she could hold her own much better. The world population of humans was spiralling out of control.

Even though it was still a controversial subject, David Attenborough was right when he said birth control was essential to bring families down to a reasonable level, and keeping the birth-rate sustainable was the single biggest factor in combating climate change and the destruction of the planet.

As she pointed this out, gently but firmly, she saw Alana give up the argument. She was a chartered certified accountant after all. She could do the maths. There was no need to personalise it, and fall out, when they were still so in love, was there? Having a baby simply wasn't logical. End of story.

Chapter 13

Over the hills and far away.

They made it into Manchester by mid-day and managed to get round the circular M60 as far as Salford in time for lunch in a café on Salford Quays, where the vast media village now dominated the water-front. It was a complete transformation of the old days when rotting cotton mills stood next to damp and sinister canals, and the whole area had become gentrified and now seemed full of BBC news presenters and chat show hosts taking their guests out to lunch.

Alana knew there was no point going to her parents' house just yet. Everyone worked, but her mother's shift at the care-home finished at 2 pm, so she reckoned they just had enough time to top up with some more Christmas presents before they drove the final two miles through narrow streets to the little terraced house where she'd grown up.

"Come on, let's go into the shopping precinct and see what we can find. I waited until now to get some toys for my nephews."

Steph nodded and fell in step with her. They'd eaten something resembling a chicken burger and chips in the local fast-food spot, but it had tasted like cardboard, and she said to Alana how she could appreciate, with hindsight, her mother's well-flavoured home cooking, and the trouble she'd gone to, just for their brief two-night stay.

The damp December air hanging over Manchester and Salford paradoxically cheered Alana up. This was her home turf, rough, gruff, but with its own brand of north-west energy. She didn't want to live in Manchester any more, but it was good to visit now and then. She dragged Steph around an outlet centre and they emerged with three or four bags of toys and

Christmas traditional treats.

"How do you know what to buy them?" asked Steph, bemused by the forensic way Alana had dived into the outlet centre stores, using her phone to check prices and look up brands.

"My sister told me. As I told you in London, this year it's all dinosaurs, and star-wars Lego. The children watch those YouTube videos on line where amateurs make the toys fight each other, and pretend to recreate Jurassic Park in their back yards. They make millions of dollars apparently, so many kids watch the videos, and then want the models. Louise told me which ones to go for. And the one you bought for my nephew Noah, that's one he'll love."

"A T-Rex which eats cars?"

"Yes, you've got a winner there. And it was discounted. We've done very well, my dear. You'll see."

"What about my idea of booking into a Premier Inn or Holiday Inn for two nights? Do you think your parents would object? And could we even get a room at this late stage?"

"Let's find out when we get home. I don't want to upset Mum if she's already catered for us, but it may help. We don't have a spare room, and only one bathroom."

"Last year, we stayed with a neighbour down the street as I remember."

"Yes, but that wasn't ideal was it?"

"No, I don't even want to go there! Remember, we could hear every sound through her wall, and we didn't dare make a squeak ourselves."

They returned to the car, and Steph sat with all the parcels on her knee, while Alana, who knew Salford, even gentrified Salford, like the back of her hand, navigated their way through a maze of identical streets to her parents' modest terraced house.

It was a world of its own, intimate, overcrowded roads with no room for the many cars which now clogged them, and row upon row of red-bricked houses. But the houses in this part were now all owner-occupied, mostly with new windows, re-roofed and painted up. The street where the Byrnes lived was alight with enthusiastic Christmas displays in most windows and round the front doors. A few plastic reindeer even galloped over the roofs.

Cath Byrne welcomed them in as soon as she heard the door-bell, and they squeezed down the narrow hallway behind her. She was still dressed in the uniform she wore at the nursing home where she worked, and her hair was falling over her eyes.

"Well, you're a sight for sore eyes! Come on in my loves, and get warm. You must be freezing."

Alana gave her mother a big kiss, and they deposited the parcels on the floor by the kitchen table as they sat down.

"How are you both? Working too hard, I daresay," said Kath over her shoulder as she put the kettle on.

"No more than you," smiled Stephanie. "How many hours are you working at the care-home these days?"

"Oh, usually no more than forty, except if someone's off sick, as they are right now. I've done three nights and three days over the last week, but I was glad of the extra cash, to help us over Christmas.

"You know Myra's Benny is being made redundant. The building trade is in the doldrums right now, because of uncertainty over Brexit, so he's being laid off at the end of the Month, and she's only got the mail sorting work until Christmas. They've brought in an agency down at the sorting office, and zero hours contracts, so she doesn't know one week to the next how much she'll earn."

Alana said quickly, "You must let me help, Mum, if things are tight. You know I want to. Just say, OK?" She looked round at the familiar shabbiness of her parent's home. Nothing had been replaced in twenty years, but it had been home to six growing children and was packed full of love and happy memories.

Cath passed them both a mug of tea, and said to Steph as she looked fondly at her eldest daughter, "You know she's our princess, don't you, the one who escaped and went off to university. The one who moved to London. But she never forgets her old mum, nor her dad and all her brothers and sisters. She never misses a birthday. Heart of gold, our Ally here."

"I know where she gets it from," replied Steph, obviously

knowing how much Cath appreciated a little compliment.

Alana changed the subject.

"Mum, we're hoping to stay tonight and tomorrow night, and drive back on Christmas Day after breakfast. The roads will be quiet then and we can get back to London easily. Is that OK? And also, how about Steph and I stay close by but not here, instead put up in one of the local hotels? I think that would make things easier for you here, wouldn't it? Hasn't Adrian moved back home? And I know you've already got Myra and Benny."

Cath was no fool. "I know you 'girls' would like your own space, and so it might be easier. But you must stay late and get here early on Christmas morning, if you're going to leave before the meal. I wish you could stay for a week, darling, like you used to. I miss you so much, but I do understand."

Alana and her mum exchanged a look, which meant they were both thinking mainly of Grandma Byrne who would be coming round for Christmas lunch as always, from her house two streets away, and who had no mixed feelings and no reticence in stating just what she thought of Alana's lifestyle. She hailed from Belfast, with the rasping heavy Northern Ireland accent, and one look from her could make the merriest little Christmas spirit want to crawl away and die.

"So let's see if we can get in somewhere at the last minute," said Alana, knowing that if her mother approved, then her dad would have no further say in the matter, and Grandma's fury could beat itself up on its own. She and Steph would have escaped intact, even before Granny had arrived.

They were in luck. The Holiday Inn down on the Salford Quays had a few rooms free for Monday and Tuesday nights, and Alana booked them by credit card over the phone. Then they settled down for some old fashioned family time with the Byrnes, several of whom would roll in shortly, as they finished their various jobs.

Alana had five younger siblings, most of whom were either married, or living with partners. The one nearest to her in age, Bridget, had defied all convention and married the son of their local mini-mart owner, a Muslim immigrant from Pakistan, but apart from not drinking, Hamid sat very lightly on the religious side of his culture, and made no demands on his Catholic wife.

Bridget had followed down the maths and science route, and now worked in a medical lab testing vaccines. They had two small boys, Hamid and Noah.

Then came Alana's two brothers, Patrick and Seamus, named after the deceased grandfathers on each side of the family. Patrick was a heating engineer, putting in boilers and updating central heating systems for a living, and happily settled in a flat with his girlfriend Sharon. Their baby, Florence was now eighteen months old, and Alana was dying to see and nurse her again. But Seamus was single and in the army, currently stationed in Germany, so as usual he wouldn't be home for Christmas.

The youngest two in the family Myra and Adrian, were both still at home. Myra had a live-in boyfriend, Benny, who was a time-served brick-layer, and Adrian, always keen on trains, was a junior manager with the railway company, based at Victoria station in the centre of Manchester. He was dating the girl who read out the station announcements over the loudspeaker above the platform.

It had taken Steph the entire three years of their relationship to get her head round all these new brothers and sisters-in-law. And she still hadn't met Seamus, a sergeant in the Royal Fusiliers.

Alana regretted it, because of all the Byrne tribe, she felt closest to Seamus. She'd been ten when he was born and he was very much her baby. The best looking, and gentlest of the boys, he had astonished her by signing up for an apprenticeship in the army when he was seventeen, but was now in his third tour of duty and would probably stay in the military until he was fifty.

Alana's family was an argumentative, and rumbustious bunch, and most of them would have fitted in very well as extras on the Coronation Street film set. In fact the studios where the soap was filmed was within whistling distance from their home. But Alana had already broken the ice years before about her uncompromising preference for her own sex, so by the time she introduced Steph to them all, most of them accepted her with open arms.

This afternoon, Steph sat down by the 'lazy man's gas fire' in the tiny sitting room, and did her share of present wrapping while Alana stayed with her mother in the kitchen and helped her prepare for the family party. She and her mother needed this time together, a precious hour or so before everyone else came home. They were peeling potatoes, ready to put them into a classic meat and potato pie, which was a Byrne family tradition in the run-up to Christmas.

Alana knew her mother had guessed something was wrong with her favorite child. Her words then came as no surprise.

"What's up, Petal? Something's not right. I can tell. Are you and Steph going through a bad patch?"

"No, it's good Mum, it's all fine. Except..."

"What?" whispered Cath, scooping up a pile of peelings and putting them into a colander to take out to the garbage bin.

Alana helped her, putting the spuds on to boil on the gas hob.

"I just miss her so much when she travels. She's been away for longer than three months this time and I nearly died of loneliness. And there's something else. I do want us to settle and have a baby, and she doesn't, not at all. I've just been talking to her about it over the weekend and she says the whole idea frightens her. Heck, I'm scared she might leave me if I keep pressing the subject."

Cath looked at her quizzically. "Well, if it's so important to you, why not do what your Aunt Siobhan did with Uncle Pete?"

"Huh? I've no idea what..."

"Get pregnant yourself and then ask her to marry you, make an honest woman of you."

"Mum! Gay relationships don't work like that. We have to be upfront and honest with each other. I wouldn't presume..."

"Well then, I guess you may end up a childless fifty-year-old. If Steph truly loves you, then there must be a good reason she's frightened of raising a child. But she shouldn't stop you having one. Besides, people don't always know what's in their own best interest."

"I'm afraid I suggested she should have the kid, while I keep working. I earn five times what she does, and I'm older. I just thought it would be more sensible if she was the first mum who carries the child, and I'm the second mum who supports it."

"And who have you lined up for the other vital ingredient for this love-nest? Who's going to be your baby's daddy?"

"We haven't even made it as far as that decision, but I suppose we could use a sperm bank."

"What?"

"Gay couples do it all the time. You can pick an ethnicity, a comparable background, education level…"

"Well, for God's sake don't let your Grandma Byrne hear you talk like that, lass. Even I would have trouble coming round to that idea. The poor wee thing would have no idea where he came from. No, love, I'm old enough to still think babies are best made naturally by a quick ten-minute fumble at the back of the bus shelter."

There was the sound of a door banging open and Alana hastily whispered. "OK, but please don't tell Dad or any of the others about what I've said. Steph and I will work it out somehow ourselves. But you're right about one thing. The bus-shelter idea would certainly be cheaper than using a sperm-bank! And don't assume our hypothetical baby will be a boy either. I'm planning on a little girl!"

Her father, Gerald, then burst into the kitchen with a crate of beer bottles in his arms. He worked as a warehouseman for a major food retailer, so could buy any of their goods at a discount, including the booze. He put down the crate and swept Alana up in a rib-crushing squeeze. "Hello, Princess, come slumming? No, don't pull that face. I'm only teasing. It's good to see you, and I suppose Steph's here as well?"

"Of course!"

"Good. I used to get tired of learning the names of all your different girlfriends."

Her father was his usual blunt self, but she took his comments on her chin. There was no viable alternative, because she had never won any verbal argument against him. He was an ex-docker, raised on Labour politics from his youth, and could talk the hind leg off a donkey. But his heart was hers, even with her weird lesbian ways, and hoity-toity London glamour. Alana knew this, and she also knew to keep her parents on her side.

Cath poured a pile of crisps into a cereal bowl and fetched down some glasses.

"Why don't you pour us all a beer and let's go into the sitting room?" So they did.

Alana saw what a sorry mess Steph had made of wrapping up the last round of presents, but at least she'd tried. She was now trying to prise the sticky tape off her fingers, and grinned up at her as if to say, "Well, you knew what a klutz I am!"

The kids would rip off the paperwork any way first thing on Christmas morning, so for now they put the labelled parcels under the artificial tree standing next to the television, and all settled down to drink beer and watch the goggle-box. If her family life resembled the *'Royale Family'* sit-com, at least it was a culture Alana understood, and could navigate her way round confidently.

Steph scooted along to the end of the sofa and let her nestle down beside her. She looked and felt wonderful. Alana thought about her mother's unexpected advice. Maybe going out and getting pregnant wasn't the most sensible advice a mother could give, but what about suggesting she propose marriage to Steph? That was something else altogether.

The very idea made a rush of adrenalin fire up her insides, and she could feel a familiar burn of arousal between her legs. If this was love, then she was definitely in it! And she cherished the feeling of Steph's Rohan-clad thigh against her own, as warm as toast! Maybe she'd been approaching all their problems in entirely the wrong way.

One by one the other three residents of the house rolled in from work, and about eight o'clock they finally sat round the kitchen table and tucked into Cath's meat and potato pie, with red cabbage and mushy peas.

"It's an old Lancashire tradition," said Alana to Steph, "From the days when there were large families and not much money to pay for meat."

"I thought you were all loyal to your Irish roots," Steph laughed. And Cath snorted.

"If we were to go to the full Irish experience, it would be potato pie, with no meat at all."

"Talking of the Irish," said Alana's dad. "Tomorrow, can you pop round and visit Ma, your Grandma Byrne. She's asked to see you especially, Ally. I can tell you've been avoiding her since last year. But you used to be her favourite, and she only lives round the corner."

Alana felt her heart sink. Yes, when she was seven, looking angelic in her first communion outfit, maybe then she had been her grandmother's darling. But after she declared at fourteen that never, never, did she intend taking the veil and gracing the family with a nun amongst its midst, their relationship had definitely cooled.

And Grandma's outrage when she had come out as gay, had scorched the pavement just as fiercely as the DeLorean time-travelling car had in that film "Back to the Future". Alana would never forget, and could not forgive, all the harsh things which had been said to her face, and certainly behind her back by that bitter old woman.

"Dad, I don't think so. I don't think I can."

"Darling, my mother's nearly ninety, and I know she regrets some of the things she said to you last year. Can't you give her a chance?"

"I don't suppose she said she wanted to meet Stephanie?"

"No, I think she just wants a quiet time with you alone. Can't you give her that? In the morning? Just half an hour or so? It would make my life easier, and maybe bring you some peace of mind. She won't be with us forever."

Alana sighed, and Steph reached across the table and squeezed her hand. "You don't have to do this, if you don't want to," she said, quietly, offering a way out. But Alana felt the vortex of her family's love pulling her back with their strong binds of family loyalty and her dad's obvious hope she'd agree.

Myra, her younger sister, who managed to live with her boyfriend under her mother's house without anyone yelling at her about her morals, gave her a sisterly nudge, and said, "Go on, Ally. If it's horrible, then at least you'll know you did your best, and don't forget you're bunking off Christmas dinner anyway. We'll have to sit through three hours of her at least, bitching on about the world and its wicked ways."

"OK," Alana sighed, feeling about twelve again, not thirty-eight and a senior executive in a large accountancy firm. She said, "I'm not afraid of Grandma any longer. She can't hurt me. Sticks and stones and all that. Dad, tell her I'll pop in for a coffee about eleven thirty tomorrow, on Christmas Eve."

Then she realized she hadn't bought a present for the old dragon. Oh well, a box of chocolates might suffice, and she could pick one up in her brother-in-law's convenience store. No point wasting cash and care on an old woman who had done her best to make her miserable.

They left the house just before ten that night, with Alana driving, as Steph had gone through quite a few cans of Guinness as they watched mindless drivel on the box. She was tipsy by the time they reached the Holiday Inn, and secured entry into the car-park next door. Alana had to take care of the check-in process and pushed her into the lift to find their room. If she could keep her awake, at least tonight might end with some fun.

The room was decorated in the bland greys and maroons of hotel interior design and seemed anonymous and cold after the rough and tumble of her family home. But Steph had been right. They could de-stress here, behave like adults. Steph clearly thought so. As soon as the door shut, she grabbed Alana and pushed her against the wall. Drunk or not, she had the right idea and Alana's happiness monitor rose by several hundred points.

Chapter 14

The wrath of Granny Byrne.

It was nearly ten before they stirred from the bed the following morning, having had a somewhat busy night, and then waking again around five for another session of making love which Alana initiated this time. She so rarely had the chance to indulge in such shenanigans, lying in beautifully pressed cotton sheets with her arms wrapped around a beautiful woman, and no need to dress for work, or brave the Victoria line with ten thousand other miserable workaholics.

Today was a real holiday, and she was determined to enjoy it. By the end of the second session she had virtually devoured Steph and thoroughly enjoyed getting her own back for the midnight ravaging she'd had. Then they slept again for a further four hours. It was positively decadent and sybaritic, and gave Alana just the physical boost she needed before she faced the wrath of Granny Byrne.

They enjoyed a coffee together in the room, after Alana had insisted she thoroughly wash out the mugs provided with the kettle on the tray. Steph smiled at her, obviously thinking this was something funny, but Alana said, "Oh, you obviously haven't seen the TV series 'Confession of hotel cleaners.' I'm taking no chances."

"Just make it hot and black," groaned Steph. "I think I rather over-did the Guinness last night."

"You did rather go for it you know. There was no need to keep my dad company pint for pint. He must have the liver of an ox."

They sat down at the little table and drank their coffee. Steph swallowed a couple of paracetamol tablets along with it, and bit into a sweet cookie from the little packet of shortbread provided on the tray.

"I think if you're visiting your grandma, you need a strategy for survival. Grannies can be trouble. Mine sadly died before she could meet you, but she may not have been any friendlier to you than yours is to me. Why gay people have to be so scared of their own families, and have to make themselves miserable trying to hide who they are so often, I'll never understand."

"Neither do I darling, neither do I. Prejudice is a terrible thing, and we just have to hang in there and fight it. I am all set now for ten rounds with Grandma, don't worry. She won't get to me, I promise."

But when they left the hotel and went back to her Salford home, Alana felt much less confident. When she was a small child she had spent many days in her grandmother's house, while her mother worked in various low-paid and unfulfilling jobs, and even when there were more children and Alana had started school, she would call in for her tea at least twice a week.

Granny Bridget Byrne had only borne sons, so she concentrated on turning Alana into her idea of Irish womanhood from an early age, teaching her to cook, and sew on buttons, and the importance of cleaning, whether it was oneself, one's clothes or one's house. "Keep yourself pure," was her most used adage, followed by "Cleanliness is next to Godliness".

Alana absorbed the second proverb into her very bones, but found the first one hard to interpret. She guessed it referred to avoiding older boys, those strange alien creatures who played football and gathered in gangs on the street corners, and until she was in her teens, thought it was a very easy commandment to keep.

But then life became much more complicated. She fell head over heels in love with Tracy Mulligan, a silly, reckless girl in her class at the local Catholic High School. Tracy had a wicked laugh, and seemed to be very sophisticated about all things to do with sex. Alana sat quietly on the edge of her gang of girlfriends as they shared outrageous stories of sex they'd had with various boys. Her personal fantasies were quite different.

They began to involve Tracy though, rather than any boys, and she was miserable with desire.

Then one afternoon, as they waited for the bus, Tracy had suddenly said, " Sod this for a lark," and grabbed Alana, pushed her up against the back wall of the bus shelter, and kissed her firmly on the mouth.

Alana, astonished, appalled, but overwhelmed with joy, just let her, and so started on a long line of lesbian encounters with girls who were almost without exception, mad, bad, and dangerous to know. Kisses in the bus-shelter evolved into explorations into her tights and then semi-naked encounters in other people's bedrooms, and behind the gym showers in the school.

Boys never became an issue. She obviously wasn't going to keep herself 'pure' for much longer, but Alana kept the myth going in her head. She was still technically a virgin. Getting pregnant would never be a problem. But her grandmother, not seeing any boys hanging around, seemed to assume she could push her into becoming a bride of Christ.

Anyway, twenty-five years on, maybe they could now settle their differences, and learn to let each other live in peace. Maybe.

Alana had relented slightly, and as well as a box of Milk-tray, she'd bought her grandmother a pretty cardigan from a shop on the Salford Quays, and now walked with the gifts round to her house. She had left Steph nursing her headache and doing research into trafficking networks across Europe on her lap-top in her parents' front room. If Steph wanted to solve the world's problems, that was great, but this morning Alana had to solve one of her own.

She covered the two hundred yards in a few minutes and then stood nervously outside her granny's front door. Her brave words to Steph seemed to have vanished, and she felt ten years old again. But this was ridiculous, so she rang the doorbell, and rapped on the knocker as well, for good measure. There was a long wait, but eventually she could see her grandmother moving slowly towards the door behind the glass, and heard the key turning in the lock and the Yale latch being pulled back as well.

The door opened and a tiny, fierce woman stared up at her, blinking against the wintry sunlight.

"Oh, it's you. Come in then, and don't let the draughts through. It's hard enough paying the heating bills as it is."

"*Nice to see you as well*," thought Alana as she shut the door behind her. It was almost as if even by coming through the front door, she had somehow offended her grandmother.

"Dad said you wanted to see me. How are you keeping, Granny?"

"Terrible, as always. Not that you'd know. I haven't seen my eldest grand-daughter for a year."

"That's because you said terrible things to me last Christmas, practically cursed me to hell. I'm not made of stone, Granny. You really hurt me."

"Oh well, maybe I let my tongue run away with me. But was there the need to take it so personally, or go off in a sulk for twelve months?"

Alana had nothing to say to that. Her grandmother was a one-off, really. She should have known there'd be no repentance, no forgiveness given or sought.

But Granny Byrne was about to give her the shock of her life. They both moved into the tiny front parlour, where the gas-fire was blasting out heat and the temperature must have been near to 80 degrees. Alana sat down on the sofa as her grandmother eased herself back into her arm-chair and put her bad leg up on a footstool.

"Still got the ulcer, I see. Your leg's no better?"

"No, keeps me awake at night. The pain is horrible, but I bear it as best I can. I keep thinking it's a punishment for all my sins."

"What sins would those be, Gran? I always thought you were second only to St Bridget in good works and attendance at Mass."

"There are sins of omission, my girl, and sins of the heart. And I've been thinking more and more over recent months, about sins I've inflicted on you in particular, some things I need to resolve."

"Me? What do you mean?"

"You were right just now. Last Christmas, as I have done

before on many occasions, I admit I said things I wish I hadn't. It's just that I've never understood how you could brazenly chase after women all your life, how bold you were, how open about it. But now I'm old I'm seeing things differently."

"How do you mean?"

"I was brought up very narrow, you know. Our Da used to get the belt out if we ever even looked at a boy, and yet he gave my poor mother thirteen children altogether, and drove her into an early grave."

"Thirteen? I never knew."

"Well, I lost four brothers and sisters when they were tiny. Scarlet fever and whooping cough. Our house in Belfast was terribly damp, and we were too overcrowded. That was one reason why I left home as early as I could and married your grandfather.

"It was hard to get work in the Belfast shipyard if you were Catholic, so we moved to England, to Liverpool, where we could both earn a decent wage. I vowed then and there I'd have no more than two children, whatever the priest said, so I just had your father and your Uncle Brendan, and then your grandfather had the operation. We kept it secret though. If the Church had found out, we'd have been in terrible trouble."

Alana was amazed at how open her grandmother was being. She had a sudden little feeling of empathy with her, and pulled out the Christmas presents she'd brought. "Here's a present for you, Granny, and some chocolates. Shall I put them over here on the sideboard? And can I make us either a coffee or a cup of tea?"

"Only if you're thirsty, dear. Thank you for the gifts, but I'd rather you simply stayed a while and let me get something off my chest."

Alana sat back down on the sofa, more intrigued by the minute.

"Alright."

"The thing is…"

"Yes?"

"I was the same."

"What do you mean?"

"I was the same as you. You know, when I was a wee young thing. Wanting the girls instead of the boys."

"Huh?"

Whatever words Alana had expected to come out of her grandmother's mouth, they certainly weren't those. She was speechless.

Her grandmother looked off into the middle distance and carried on, with a sad intensity to her voice.

"I never knew it was normal, or that any other girl might feel these things. I thought I was wicked even to have the thoughts. No-one ever sat me down and told me it wasn't just me, that there were others, that there were many women in the world who lived with other women and loved them quite freely. In my day, in our community, it was never discussed.

"So I buried it all, so deep I thought it had curled up and died inside me. But then I had two or three terrible experiences as an adult in my forties and fifties, where I fell in love and had to fight so hard not to show it. I've never told anyone, ever, before now."

The bombshell exploded right inside Alana's mind. She couldn't believe what she was hearing.

"But then, if that's the way it was, why were you so harsh with me, when you could, you could have helped me so much when I was growing up?"

"I know, and I'm ashamed. I really am, now. I saw myself in you so clearly. And when you were about sixteen, and I was in my late sixties, I had the worst experience in my life. My lovely friend Anne, whom I had loved so very much for more than twenty years, but was never able to acknowledge as anything more than a friend, went and committed suicide, took her own life.

"I knew I'd killed her, by refusing to tell her the truth and let her love me. She finally confessed she loved me, you see, not just as a friend, and I was very harsh with her, pushed her away. She thought she was at fault, that she'd misread the signs. So she went and did that, took an overdose in her despair. And I knew it was all my fault. Because I did love her, with all my heart.

"And about the same time, there was you. You, you with

your sweet innocent happiness at your new girlfriend, and I was just so jealous and filled with self-hate I turned on you instead of myself. All this time, I've been blaming you for your honesty, your courage, and your happiness. I've resented you the freedom you grasped to live the life you wanted, and I wanted to punish you. I am so very, very sorry, Alana. I truly am."

Alana felt the tears welling up in her eyes. She moved forward and knelt at her grandmother's knee, taking her hands and putting her head down in her lap. She couldn't speak at all for several moments, then as she felt her Granny's small hand come up and smooth her hair, she said quietly, "You've no idea what those words mean to me."

"Can you ever find it in your heart to forgive me, darling girl?"

"Of course. And I understand why you never came out. They were such different times, you had all your religion as well, bearing down on you."

"Yes, but that's no excuse. I married Grandpa Byrne under a lie, just to escape from home."

"But if you hadn't, then I and all your other grandkids wouldn't be here. Think about that! The past is the past. Nothing can alter it, but maybe we can at least move forward in the future."

"I can't tell your father or mother, or anyone else. I'm ashamed of so much, but I don't want your Dad to think I didn't want or love him."

"No, I understand. But can I bring Steph round to meet you again, maybe later? I'd like to share you with her, and she doesn't even have a granny of her own anymore."

Alana looked up at the sad and burdened old woman, and they exchanged smiles, the first time she could ever remember her grandmother looking at her with undeniable approval. She eventually stood up and went back to her seat on the sofa.

"But did something trigger your decision to tell me? What's changed?"

"I watched the programme on the television, "Gentleman Jack". It was about a woman in the nineteenth century who dressed like a man and wanted to marry a girl, and I started watching it by mistake. But then it really got to me, and I could see that women like us have been there all along, often hidden away. But they are all out there anyway, hiding in plain sight. I realized what damage I'd done, to my friend Anne, to myself, and now to you. Can you ever forgive me?"

"You've already asked me that, Granny. Of course I forgive you, and I want to thank you as well."

"Why ever?"

"I've inherited my gayness from you. And this makes me so happy. I wouldn't be me without you. I just never knew!"

"I think I might manage a cup of coffee now. I feel all talked out."

"Right, I'm on it," and Alana jumped up and went through to the back kitchen to fill the kettle. The normality of getting together a mug and the bone china cup and saucer her grandmother still liked to use, of putting in a spoonful of instant coffee and stirring in the hot water helped steady her nerves. But Alana had never been so shaken in her life. Everything she had understood about the way things were in her tiny corner of the universe had just been turned upside down. Granny Byrne was gay. Whoever would have thought it!

Chapter 15

The giving of gifts.

It was 3pm on Christmas Day, and the roads into London were virtually deserted. Most of the British population were probably hunkered down, full of turkey and Christmas pudding, sitting in semi-alcoholic stupors around their televisions, waiting for the Queen's Christmas broadcast.

Steph knew this was probably the case for her Sheffield family, as well as the folk they had left in Manchester that morning. Whether Alana's folks would bother to watch Her Majesty, she wasn't so sure, as the vein of republican sentiment ran deep through their culture.

But in any case, she felt a deep sense of relief that between them they had navigated the Christmas holiday period, and it had been good, far better than in previous years, and a lot of that was down to her being less screwed up, more mature.

It had been joyous in fact, with all the kids playing with their dinosaurs and Cath pink and tipsy with the Baileys Alana had bought her. Now that they had been so reconciled with Granny Byrne Steph felt sad they hadn't been able to stay for lunch, but that hadn't been the plan and the house was full of people, and children.

Maybe she was growing up at last, and letting people be who they were, not being so self-conscious and imagining everyone was judging her all the time. Steph realized she had spent most of her life feeling insecure and inadequate, and it had spoiled her relationships all around. It had made her self-centred.

Then on Christmas Eve, Alana's astounding revelations about her granny, and then the surreal experience of being invited round to the feared and dreaded woman's house herself, to sit down and be asked all about herself, to be approved of, even joked with, had been more than the icing on the cake. It had been an enormous slice of fruit cake, with cherries, topped with marzipan.

She could tell that Granny Byrne was still nervous and shy about talking about her own experiences, but coming out to Alana had opened a dam deep inside her heart, and she wanted to be real. She needed to tell her story to people she could trust to understand it. And she had certainly done that. Such a tragic tale it had been too.

But then, just before they left, to return to the family party back around the corner, as she showed them out, the old soul had said something else, which had shaken Steph to the core.

"Don't be afraid to take risks, girls. Don't be like me, and limit your life to a small terraced house in Salford, with only bitter memories of loss for company. I know some gay women even get married these days and have kids. I'd like to see Alana give me a great-grandchild one day before I die. Please don't hold back on my account. If you do get married, I'll come to your wedding and I'll throw confetti. I promise."

Steph was still dwelling on those words. Alana was driving them now, for the second leg of their journey south, and she looked across at her lover's beautiful grey eyes and ash-blonde hair, imagining how she'd look in a wedding dress.

Alana hadn't referred to her grandmother's promise since, but Steph could tell she was thinking about it as much as she was. It had put yet another stone in the outwardly calm mill-pond of their life, and the ripples were circling out in all directions.

If they were to get married, she decided, she would do the proposing, and only after the decision was made, did she realize how radically her compass bearings had changed. Steph wasn't phobic about being tied down anymore. She knew she was committed to Alana, more than she had thought possible. She didn't just want a girl-friend any more. She wanted a fiancée, wearing her ring. Damn it, she wanted a wife!

Their flat seemed warm and welcoming when they returned to it an hour later, and after all the various households they'd visited over the last five days, it was good simply to sit together on the sofa, glasses of red wine in their hands and old slippers on their feet. They switched on the lights on Alana's little tree, and then just enjoyed the relief of surviving their Christmas road trip, and making it home with their bodies and partnership intact.

They had left the exchange of their own presents until now, when they could share them in the quiet of their own home. Ally handed over a beautifully wrapped box, and inside all the tissue paper, Steph found a delicate grey cashmere polo sweater, so soft against her hands, and something she could wear in the coldest, dampest months of the year. It was a change from her scientifically designed normal Rohan gear, but she loved it. It was like a wearable cuddle.

"Don't fling it in the washing machine," cautioned Ally. "If in doubt give it to me and I'll hand-wash it for you. It needs gentleness, not speed."

Steph grinned," You know me so well. Here is my present for you, anyway. I hope you like it. It's a similar throw-back to the pre-digital age."

She watched as Ally unwrapped the slim little box, which the guy in the specialist shop had luckily wrapped up so neatly for her. Then she enjoyed the look on Alana's face as she drew out a top of the range fountain pen, crystal blue, with a gold nib.

"It's beautiful. But it must have cost hundreds. You shouldn't have."

"Yes I should. I know you do most of your work on the screen, but you have to sign off your reports and audits by hand, and this will do that for you. Every time you do that, I want you to think of me."

"I certainly will do that, darling. Thank you, it's beautiful." They sat back together, contented, and just enjoyed the moment.

But then the silence was broken by the shrill buzz of the landline telephone. Alana looked so settled and tired, in a good way though, that Steph leaned back and lifted the phone off its cradle. She expected it to be one of their mothers calling to make sure they were home safely. But it wasn't.

A sudden burst of cosmic energy entered their lives.

"Hi, you called before Christmas, about a girl on a plane

from Kinshasa."

"Yes, I did. Who is this? Do you know who she is?"

"I think I do. It sounds as though it might have been Leontine, one of my former school girls, from Goma, where I have been teaching for twenty years, in the DRC. I'm Sister Jennifer Mary, calling from Montreal. We were on retreat, but I came back early. I can only cope with so much silence. Where are you, and where is Leontine? I'm really astounded to hear you saw her travelling on a plane to Brussels."

Steph waggled her eyebrows at Alana and put the phone onto loudspeaker, so she could listen in as well. She told the story of her encounter with the young girl, to this woman religious in Canada, and then said, "I thought she asked me to call her sister, but if what she was saying was to call you Sister, then it might make sense. I'm worried she is in danger. She seemed very scared, and certainly not happy. She appeared to be a maid or a nursemaid to the family she was travelling with."

"That may have just been a ruse, to get her through immigration without notice. They often do that. Was there a man with her as well?"

"Yes, an older guy, about forty, with a scar on his cheekbone. She seemed really scared of him."

"Sonny Alvares. Nasty piece of work. He'd been hanging about the school looking for the girls without family, the scholarship students. I knew he was very bad news."

There was a pause, and then the woman came through again, stronger and more determined than before.

"Listen, I'm going to send you a picture of Leontine I have on my phone. She's in a group of girls. I won't tell you which one she is, but if you can identify her and tell me if she's in the group and which one she is, then I'm coming over to London straight away. I can't do anything from here."

Steph sat upright and paid close attention. "Yes, I'm waiting. Send me the picture to my mobile phone, my cell phone. Let me give you the number."

She dictated the number, and then put down the land-line phone, opening up her cell-phone. It rang almost at once, and she continued her conversation with the Canadian. "I can remember the young woman very clearly. I am sure I would recognize her."

Then there was a ping on Messenger, and an image emerged. Steph opened it and stared hard at the images of five young girls all smiling broadly at the camera. Her recent acquaintance was certainly there, right in the middle. She briefly showed the picture to Alana and then spoke to the caller. "Yes, I'm afraid it is her. She's the middle one in the group."

There was a quick intake of breath, as if the caller was suddenly shocked and took in the implications of what she'd just had confirmed.

"Expect me tomorrow in the morning if I can find a flight. If you are up for it, you can help me look for her and get her out of whatever mess she'd in. We can go back to Brussels and pick up her trail. It's only six days old."

Steph chuckled. Here was a woman after her own heart. "Yeah, we'd like that. We're free until January 2nd anyway. Do you speak French…?"

"Of course I do, I'm French-Canadian. Can I come to your place? Can I have your address? Is it far from Heathrow? I'm sorry, I still don't know your name."

"I'm Steph Hunter, and my partner is Alana Byrne."

"Oh," – there was a definite pause here, "So you live with a woman?"

"Yes, is that a problem?" Steph heard her voice rise defensively.

"Not at all. Give me her cell-phone number as well as this one and I'll call you both to let me know my flight details."

"One of us can meet you at Heathrow. That will be much easier for you. I'm so happy to know someone cares about her … she's called Leontine, you say?"

"Yes, after my mother. I am so grateful for your quick-thinking, and for your persistence in tracking me down."

"No, thank you, Sister, for solving the first of the mysteries. We now have a name for the person we are seeking."

"Don't bother with the Sister. Call me Jenni. I should be with you tomorrow morning. 'Bye."

And she was gone.

"Wow," said Alana. "Mystery solved, do you suppose?"

"Sounds like it. But I am sure it won't be easy, finding her on the continent. It will be like looking for a needle in a haystack. Are you up for a little adventure though? I didn't ask before I agreed we would go with her, but it would be so great if you can come with us. We'll achieve more if there are three of us, and besides. I don't want to leave you right now, even for a few days."

Alana hesitated for one moment, and then said, "Yes, of course I'm game. I'll come. Let me go and book three tickets on the Eurostar to Brussels for Friday morning."

So they were about to host a nun called Jenni. That was something to think about!

Chapter 16

Energy and purpose.

The moment she saw a tall white woman with a short pepper and salt crop of hair and a firm, brisk look about her, striding through the Terminal Three arrivals gate, Alana knew the whole dynamic of their search for the girl from the Congo was going to take a turn for the better.

Energy and purpose were written all over their new friend's demeanour, and Ally's scribbled card saying, "Sister Jenni" was redundant, as the woman immediately identified her through the crush of people meeting family and friends by the metal link barrier. She waved cheerfully and walked round to meet Alana, pulling a small carry-on navy suitcase, and with a small rucksack on her shoulder.

"Hi, you must be Steph! This worked well, didn't it? I was so pleased I managed to get a flight from Toronto late last night, and with the five hours' time difference, I seem to have missed most of the dreary public holiday."

Ally stepped up and went to pick up her suitcase, but the women brushed away her attempts to help.

So she said, "Actually I'm not Steph, but Alana Byrne, her partner. Only one of us could come to fetch you as my car's a two-seater. Steph stayed home and is cooking dinner today, so we can feed you properly. Did you get some sleep on the flight coming over?"

"Enough. I managed an hour or two, and watched a couple of films I've not seen before."

"So, is it Sister Jennifer Mary or just Jenni?" Alana was keen to get it right.

"Either. I was christened Jennifer Mary, but my friends call me Jenni or Jen."

Jenni, as Alana decided to call her, was slightly androgynous in appearance, very small busted, long-legged, wearing jeans, boots, and a black leather jacket. She was probably about fifty, though she might have been some years older or younger. Her face was very weathered and she had a tan deeper than Steph's. But her smile was roguish and she certainly didn't look pious.

"Funny kind of nun," thought Alana, mentally adjusting her brain away from the expected black or grey habit, a pink, round face behind rimless glasses and nun's head-covering. Her convent education still left a residue of sensitivity to the sisterhood, whether positive or negative she wasn't sure. But this woman had one thing she hadn't expected. Alana's gaydar immediately identified her as a member of their team. Celibate or not, Jenni was undoubtedly gay. It took one to know one.

Alana led the way back to her car, in a short-stay car-park just across from the terminal building. December 26th, Boxing Day in the UK, was a day for family and endless sporting events, or for recovering from all the festivities of Christmas Day. Heathrow was relatively quiet, but the access roads were always piled up with traffic, and the flight schedule was half as busy as normal.

"How far to your place?" Jenni had a slight French accent, but spoke English with just a faint Canadian inflection.

"An hour at least, I'm afraid. We live in Brixton, in South London. I'll take you in through the suburbs from the M25. Close your eyes and sleep if you want to."

"Certainly not. I want to get to know you, and find out more about why you are going out of your way to help my Leontine."

"*Your* Leontine? So you know her well?"

"Yes, I am sure the girl on the plane is one of my foster daughters. I've taught in DRC and before that, in Rwanda, for more than thirty years, and lately I was Principal of my community's school in Goma. Leontine was orphaned by the war, and I have fostered her, along with several others since she was tiny. I was terrified something bad would happen to her when I was forced to leave, and it looks like my fears were fully justified. I haven't heard anything from her for more than three weeks, which is most unlike her."

"Yes, she probably hasn't a phone with her anymore. So why did you return to Canada? It sounds like it wasn't your choice."

Jenni shook her head and grunted under her breath. "No, it certainly wasn't. But I've had recurring bouts of malaria nearly every year for more than a decade, and the last recent attack nearly killed me. My blood count went right down and my liver almost conked out.

"The powers that be shipped me home, and one of the most annoying aspects of taking vows as a member of a religious community, is that you're supposed to obey those in authority, however much you disagree with them. I had to be dragged kicking and screaming on to the plane.

"And now, I have even worse news from the damn medics. They say I must stay away from the tropics for life. My world has ended as I knew it. I've almost decided to leave my fellow sisters and quit the order."

"But if you go back to Africa, won't you almost certainly die?"

"Hmm, not such a bad idea, as I look at it. I was seriously thinking of shooting myself until I got your message, except that I don't think God would approve."

Alana decided to argue with her. "But surely it would be better to live and enjoy another possible thirty years of life. Who knows what sort of a future we're facing? Wouldn't it be better to contribute to it, someone with your obvious energy and gifts?"

They entered the suburbs of southwest London, and headed east towards inner-city Brixton. Jenni had gone rather quiet, and Alana wondered if she'd overstepped the mark. But after a few minutes reflection, she said, "Maybe you've got a point. Anyway, your email message fired me up, and I decided to make a break for it. December in Quebec can be pretty cheerless."

"Did the Convent give you permission and pay for your flight?"

Jenni chuckled. "Not exactly, but I signed myself out, and I have access to plenty of funds. No-one will be surprised, and I expect they will be happy not to have to look at my grumpy face for a while."

Then she paused. "But tell me about yourself. Alana Byrne, now that's a good old-fashioned Irish name. Were you raised Catholic? You don't strike me as someone filled with missionary zeal. How did you get yourself mixed up with someone who arrived on a flight from Kinshasa less than a week ago?"

So Alana started to talk. Whether it was the confident seniority of the woman in her passenger seat, or her clear-eyed, weather-beaten face, or the fact that she was a nun, but Alana ended up telling her far more about herself, and about Steph and what they meant to each other, than she had intended.

By the time they arrived back at the flat, Jenni had been given a pretty thorough account of the ties and tensions binding the women's partnership and also an insight into Alana's heart. Now it was time for her to meet Steph.

Steph had decided to cook something with a West African beat to it, to make their visitor feel at home, so a generous pan of ground-nut stew was in the electric slow-cooker, and she had tossed in a handful of dried chilli flakes for good measure. Not too many, because she knew Alana's palette was far more sensitive than hers, which had been abused for so long, it just swallowed anything these days. She had lit the lamps and turned the heating up, so when she heard the car pull up outside their window, and went to open the door, she could welcome the visitor into a warm and welcoming place.

"Come in, I'm so pleased to see you!" she said. "We thought we were looking for a needle in a haystack, but now I feel we've got the help of a person with a metal detector at least!"

"More than that," said Alana, shaking off her jacket. "Jenni here says the girl, Leontine, is virtually her daughter."

So they welcomed Jenni in together, taking her jacket and hanging it up in the hall closet and bringing her into their cosy sitting-room. The three women talked to each other, exchanging information and ideas, and later they sat down to supper and devoured Steph's spicy stew and spinach side-dish, made to resemble the cassava leaf greens of West Africa. Jenni looked happier and more animated as the evening progressed, but also more concerned and alarmed that the girl Steph had met, now identified as her Leontine, had been kidnapped and trafficked to Europe.

"She's not yet sixteen, a virgin. We have to move fast to find her and rescue her from the clutches of the men I think must have her. They could break her very easily. She knows nothing of the world outside the Congo."

Steph laid out the clues they had so far, the significance of Brussels as the girl's destination, the list of anti-trafficking people who might help in Belgium, the information she had already researched about the sex-trade and the gangs who exploited young girls. Jenni also had contacts in Brussels and suggested she call them straight away.

"The sex trade is a curse, as old as humanity. I know all about it. I worked with a remarkable couple of women some years ago on the same problem. Have you come across them? Isabel Bridgford and Carrie Monterini?"

Steph nearly fell off her chair. "Bel's my boss, and my great role model. But Carrie, her partner, did you not hear what happened to her? She was shot dead three years ago in Moldova, tracking down one of the gangs who lure young women into sex-work."

Jenni looked completely shocked, to the point of not seeming able to breathe, and then her eyes filled with tears. "Oh, no! I never knew. So poor Bel, how has she survived? She lived for that woman."

The others were astonished she knew Isabel so well. Alana took up the story and filled Jenni in with the events of the last twelve months, of Isabel's depression, her nearly fatal car accident, and then eventual recovery and new love with her medical student assistant, Bryony through the previous summer.

"They got married just after the General Election. They are still on honeymoon. But we must reintroduce you as soon as they come back to London. Bel will love to meet you again, I know."

"Everyone in the world seems to know Bel," commented Steph. "My friend in Sheffield knows her too."

"Well, she is world-famous. It's only because I've been living off the grid deep in the Congo rain-forest for the last few years that I lost touch and never heard about her loss. I am so sorry to hear it, but delighted she found happiness. She was so driven the time I knew her, never still.

"Anyway, back to the task at hand. Would it be OK if I used your phone to call my colleagues in Goma, to tell them my suspicions are right, and ask how they could have ever let her be taken? Then, when do we leave for Brussels? Do I have time to take a shower?"

Alana nodded, "By all means go ahead. You might use Skype or Zoom as well if you prefer. We have full connectivity here. It's just a sore point that Ms. Hunter here forgets to use it sometimes!"

Jenni looked across at Steph fondly as if she sympathized with her. "It's harder than you think to keep in touch across continents. Don't be too hard on her."

"Oh, well," sighed Alana, "Anyway, I've booked three tickets on the Eurostar from St Pancras station tomorrow morning, so you will have plenty of time to shower, and also stay here for the night. Our sofa converts into quite a comfy guest bed if you don't mind sleeping here in the lounge. We only have one bedroom."

"Sure, that will be fine, honey. It makes sense. I'm too impetuous at times, sorry."

Steph beamed at her. "I'm going to like you, Jenni, I know I will. At last, I won't be the craziest woman in the room! Ally here will see how sensible and restrained I am in comparison. So let's set our alarms for seven tomorrow. The train leaves at 9.30, and we have to be there early to go through security."

Jenni's call to her friends in Goma confirmed her worst fears. They told her that as soon as the boarding school broke up for the Christmas holidays, which were the main annual break for students in West Africa, Leontine had come with news that a distant cousin or "Auntie" as people tended to call all older female relations had said she was sick and needed her to nurse her.

The fifteen-year-old, starved of all affection from anyone related to her, had seemed enthusiastic that someone had contacted her, and also said she felt obliged to go. She had pushed her few clothes into a bag and boarded an overnight bus for the long trip to the Western Region, but since then, no-one had heard from her. Whether "Auntie" existed or not, no-one could confirm. She had been absent for two full weeks now.

Jenni was furious. "You should have checked it with me first!" But it was clear that once away from the campus, especially in vacation time, she had lost authority over the house-mothers in charge of the girls' boarding unit. When she put the phone down, she looked quite distressed, and her eyes even watered. She was such a tough cookie Steph didn't imagine that happened too often.

Steph picked up a freshly opened bottle of red wine, and poured Jenni a large glass. "Here, have this. It's Merlot and very smooth. It will make things look better. And I'm convinced we will find and rescue your girl. I know I talked to her on that plane for a reason."

Steph spoke with confidence and internally felt the same way. She didn't normally give much weight to intuition, or any other-worldly premonitions, but in this case, she was prepared to go with her deepest feminine instincts.

Alana put it even more theologically. "Hey, here we are, three wise women. We're not following a star, but setting off together on a quest, nevertheless. It's a good project for Epiphany, and we'll succeed, I'm sure of it."

Like Steph, it was clear Alana wanted to comfort Jenni, and give her assurance that they would support her all the way. Between them they finished the bottle, and then delved into the various boxes of chocolates they'd received as part of the presents' cache from both their families.

By 10 pm, they were all ready to turn in, and the girls left Jenni to sleep on their put-up bed which Alana had made with fresh linen, and a very cozy pure down duvet. They retreated into their bedroom and rolled into bed together. The nearness of the other room made it sensible to whisper.

Steph held Alana tight against her chest and kissed her

above the collar of her pyjamas.

"What do you think? I was rather worried when she said she was a nun…"

"Hmm, no worries there. She's of a Post Vatican II second generation. Nuns these days are real people, just like you and me. When I was a child I used to think they were kept in a cupboard in the classroom. We saw nothing of their community or private life in those days. They seemed scarcely human.

But Jenni is quite different, a fascinating woman. Clever, caring …and one important asset for our purposes, she's bi-lingual in English and French. It will make getting round Belgium, or even France if the trail leads there, so much easier for us."

"You're right, Ally. I like her a lot, too. Cuddle me for a bit, can you? This may be our last chance for a while, especially if we all have to share a room later."

Alana turned, and let Steph smother her against the pillows and cover her with kisses. Steph smiled happily in the dark, and began to undo the demure pyjama jacket under her hand. She thought again how very much she loved Alana, and how what they had was just far too good to lose. Her hasty words, when she had said her career was the most important thing in the world to her, like her vocation, now seemed seriously out of step with how she felt, and with what Ally deserved.

Then she felt Alana's arms dive under her tee-shirt top and her manicured nails rake her back, as the woman moaned softly under her kisses. And any sensible thoughts left her mind entirely.

They moved together instinctively, knowing where to kiss and tickle, knowing just what excited and pleased the other. Steph may not have played the field with many women, but she knew how truly happy being in bed with Alana made her feel. Above all else, deeper than being aroused or excited, it made her feel safe.

Chapter 17

Brussels calling.

The next morning Alana jumped out of bed when the alarm buzzed at 6am, and had coffee and tea both brewed within ten minutes. She was fired up by the thought of a trip across the channel, not having left the UK for months, but her old-fashioned thriftiness drove her to make and wrap three egg sandwiches, and fill a thermos with hot coffee. The platform food at St Pancreas wouldn't be inedible, but she balked at the thought of the prices.

The others joined her before long, and by seven, even though it was still pitch dark outside, they were out of the flat and heading for the Victoria Line tube station, half a mile down the road. The Underground would take them through to Kings Cross/St Pancras and because it was still the Christmas holidays, the train was quiet. Brixton was the end of the line, so they easily found seats together, and space for their carry-on cases.

Rising steadily up the two long escalators they emerged close to the Eurostar section of St Pancras railway station, a massive Victorian structure almost the size of a small town, and with modernized platforms, escalators and walkways for passengers taking the train route under the English Channel to Paris, Lille or Brussels, and to cities and towns across the east and north of the country.

All around them were bistros serving fresh Italian coffee, and classic French pastries, as well as a huge selections of other tempting breakfast foods, and a long row of shops, offering books, perfume, chocolate and fancy clothes, very similar to the Gare du Nord at the end of the line in Paris. But Alana had bought tickets for Brussels and this was the next train due to leave. They now needed to pass through security, and passport control, with Jenni, as a Canadian, needing to join a different line from the others.

Although the UK had not yet left the European Union, the free passage in and out of Europe was still a precious privilege to Steph, who deeply regretted she might lose it very shortly. She couldn't see one advantage of the deeply divisive Brexit.

At a time when the world needed to work together to tackle climate change and all the other serious challenges, for Britain to want to divorce itself from its twenty-seven nearest neighbours seemed the height of madness. But the Brexiteers had won the election and she, who had been battling on the subject for more than three years now, was weary of it.

They reunited with Jenni on the other side of the security and border checks and then went up to the platform to find their seats on the train. It was packed with travellers, but their seats were together, with Jenni sitting opposite them across a table. Alana straight away pulled out her flask of black coffee and a packet of egg sandwiches.

"So that's what you were up to at 6 this morning," teased Steph. "I might have known." But then she produced three muesli bars from her pocket. "Extra rations, in case we need them."

"You're treasures, both of you," remarked Jenni. "I could do with people like you two around me all the time."

Alana smiled with pleasure and unwrapped the foil parcel. "Here, have some of these then. I made three sandwiches, one for each of us. The food in the station forecourt restaurants is good, but you can easily spend £30 without realizing it."

They settled down and enjoyed the food. The train was filling up, and then on the dot of 8.30 am, it glided into movement and slid away from the platform.

"Now, tell me what you two plan to do," said Alana, as she ate her sandwich. "Where are we going first?"

Jenni said, "I have an old friend, a colleague I used to work alongside, in Brussels. I emailed her last night and she has invited us round to stay at her place for a few nights. She works for a refugee agency in the city, and they are connected to a wide range of similar groups and agencies. The contact names you gave me last night, from your associate in Sheffield, she's very familiar with them.

"The only problem may be the winter holiday. Everyone has shut down, but if we push hard enough, I think we can pull a few people from their beds to help us. I also know enough about Sonny Alvarez to get on the trail to find out if he's in the city and if he still has Leontine."

"But what about the family she was travelling with?"

"I'm sure that was just a ruse. He'd have offered her to them to help with their luggage, so she could pass through the passport control unnoticed. He'd have fixed up papers for her before they even left the Congo. He'll have also spun her some story about the sick relative having moved to Belgium. When she was in my care, she certainly didn't have a passport, just an identity card as a minor. I think he'll have put her on a false passport and added a few years to her age."

"It seems a lot of trouble to go to, and not cheap."

"No, but a young fresh girl, with no STDs, even a virgin, - she could earn him as much as a 100,000 euros in the next two to three years. Then he, or the people he sells her to, will dump her, or sell her on down the line, until she ends up working on the streets on Amsterdam, or even Manchester or Sheffield. By then she'll probably be addicted to coke or heroin as well, simply to stay able to get through each day. Some of these girls are expected to serve up to thirty men a night. One every twenty minutes."

Steph shuddered. "I can't believe men would behave like that. They must know what they're doing to the girls, that it's not free will."

"Availability, anonymity, basest physical instincts, you'd be surprised. And the wealthier and more successful the man, the more they think it's their right to buy sex. The pimps also show them respect, make them feel big men."

"Well, Leontine is somewhere in Europe, and we are going to rescue her, however hard it is. But then what? How can we get her back to England safely?"

"I don't think that will be possible. Your immigration laws

are so punitive now, it will be very hard to get her into the UK begin with, and besides, she doesn't speak English."

Jenni folded her sandwich wrapper into a tiny ball of foil and lobbed it over into a waste bin between the opposite seats.

"The best thing is for me if we can find her and she's fit to travel, to take her home to the Congo, find her strong and reliable foster parents there and re-enroll her back into our High School. She may be traumatized, but I hope, once she's back among familiar surroundings with teachers and boarding house matrons who care about her, she'll recover and finish her schooling."

Alana protested, "That sounds fine, on paper, but didn't we hear you say yesterday, you were told you couldn't go back to the Congo?"

"That was medical advice, not legal. I still have a multi-entry visa in my passport." Jenni met her gaze and pulled a face as she admitted she'd already thought this through.

"Oh, yes, I agree. It's foolish. But I promise I won't stay long. If all goes according to plan, I'll have to drag myself home again to boring old Quebec."

"Don't do that," said Steph spontaneously. "Whatever happens this week, you should come back to the UK and stay with us. Join up with Isabel and the rest of us at R.A. We'd love to have you, and with your French, you'd be a real asset. You could take over the management of all the Francophone projects, so I wouldn't need to struggle with my very basic language skills anymore in communicating with partners and reading and responding to reports."

Jenni looked stunned at the suggestion. "Well, thanks. It's certainly something to think about. It might suit me down to the ground."

"Can you get a furlough or something, remission from your convent to do it?" asked Alana.

"You mean, time off for good behaviour? Probably. Times have changed. They no longer lock us in. And the Mother Superior, who was a postulant with me back in 1980, she knows only too well how the contemplative life doesn't suit me. I've given forty years to that Order, and at fifty-eight, I think I need some freedom. I'm sure I can cut some sort of deal with her."

The winter morning was lightening all the time outside their train windows and the speed picked up as they began to travel through the North Kent countryside. Rows of houses were flashing by too fast to notice the details, but they could see the coloured lights on many roofs and the general Christmas twinkle of various illuminations as they passed through the circle of dormitory towns south of London. As the conurbations grew less busy, green fields and gentle uplands appeared, but within only a few minutes it seemed as though the British side of the Eurostar journey was drawing to a close, after the small station of Ebbsfleet.

Steph looked out of the window. "Hey, we're about to go into the tunnel. Next stop France, and then Belgium!" And the train lights came on. As the carriages all moved to artificial lighting, they began the long gentle descent below the Channel. Twenty or more miles of darkness now awaited them.

A Girl on the Plane

Chapter 18

Brussels and beyond.

It seemed a minor miracle but the Eurostar used such high speed trains across northern France to Lille and then over the border north-east to Brussels, that within two and a quarter hours of leaving London, the three 'detectives' were disembarking in Brussels South station, and were all set to plunge into the Capital of Belgium, and the centre of all things European Union. They gathered up their luggage and re-buttoned their coats. Belgium looked just as chilly and damp as London, and the grey skies were equally forbidding.

"You must know Brussels well," commented Alana, winding a long scarf around her neck several times and putting on her gloves, as they walked with everyone else down the platform to the exit barriers.

Jenny replied, "Yes, I've been here many times, and studied here when I was a young nun, preparing to go to West Africa back in the early Eighties. Do you need Euros, by the way? There's an ATM over there if you want to stock up."

"It might not be a bad idea, though we can generally pay by plastic in most places," said Steph, so they followed her suggestion and drew cash of a hundred euros each. Jenni seemed to have a bank debit card, like everyone else, and her religious constrictions seemed loose in the extreme by traditional standards, irksome as she found them.

Then, with Jenni leading the way, they hurried through the busy station to the Metro platforms below. Jenni quickly bought a strip of tickets from a machine in the station, handed some over to each of the others, and then they went through more barriers into the Underground network.

It took twenty-five minutes going north-east until they

emerged at a station close to the European Union diplomatic quarter, where all the shining glass buildings and wide-open spaces of the institutional buildings gleamed in the wintry sunshine. But Jenni turned north away from the opulent avenues towards a very different set of streets, Saint-Josse-ten-Noode, the poorest, and most densely populated of all the Brussels municipalities.

Steph and Alana simply scurried behind her as she strode purposefully forward, crossing several boulevards and walking for a quarter of a mile through the narrow streets. Then, finding the address she wanted, and running up a few steps to a large front door, she pressed her finger on the fourth button of a column of seven nameplates set against an old and tall nineteenth-century tenement building.

A female voice rang out, and Jenni answered in French. Then the door clicked and when she pushed against it, it opened to let them all inside. The entrance hall was tiled in a typically Flemish design, black and white squares, which made Steph feel for a moment she was entering an interior by Vermeer. There were some bicycles propped up in the hallway, and from four floors above them, a woman's voice rang cheerfully out.

"Cheries! Bien-venue! Ascendez, s'il vous plait!" and, taking the hint, they picked up their cases and started to climb the stairs. The apartment building didn't boast a lift, and each flight was long, with fifteen steep steps, but the old building had a faded elegance to it, and Alana especially appreciated the curve of the bannisters and original stone staircase. It had been well used, because the marble had been worn down in the centre on each tread. She wondered how many thousands of feet had run up and down these stairs since they were installed.

When they finally arrived up on the fourth floor, a short woman with bright white hair and amazingly clear blue eyes rushed out of her apartment and warmly embraced them all, kissing Jenni on both cheeks and then repeating the greetings to the others, as Jenni slightly breathlessly introduced them.

"Sophie here taught me most of what I know about Brussels. She was a great mentor to me, when I first arrived. Sophie, meet my friends Stephanie and Alana, or Steph and

Ally. ”

Sophie beamed at Jenni's two companions. "I'm sorry. My English is so old, how you say, crusty?"

"Rusty?" suggested Steph. "Don't worry at all. Parlez-vous Francais s'il vous plait. It's not a problem - We'll follow along."

Sophie beamed and ushered them into her small sitting-room. Steph and Alana were both stunned by how stacked it was with bookcases full of magazine files and reports. A large desk was covered in printed material and a large computer dominated its central area, with an old printer next to it. Posters filled the walls, all advertising women's events, the International Year of the Refugee, and a large number of faces of young people, from all over the world, including more than a dozen young Africans.

Whatever Sophie did in this room, it clearly wasn't sitting around watching daytime television with her feet up. She gathered up some piles of paperwork and made room for each of them to sit down. The English women listened as Sophie and Jenni embarked on a spirited conversation, with the Belgian lady occasionally expressing huge shock and concern and then nodding as though she clearly saw what course they should take.

"Did you follow that?" asked Jenni. "I've retold Sophie our story, and she even remembers Leontine when she taught at our school. Leontine was then just a child, ten years of age. She is shocked to hear what might have happened to her, but is not surprised.

"Sophie knows someone in the vice squad of the local police force who can probably find out if Leontine has been brought into the city and where she might be housed. The Christmas vacations aren't helping, but they may also mean the criminals haven't put her to work yet. Everyone takes time off until New Year, even the traffickers."

"So, is she going to make some calls?" asked Steph. "What can we do? Surely there's something? Now we're here I want to be pro-active."

Her instincts of rushing in like a fool were in danger of

running away with her, she knew that, but now they were probably in the same country as the little waif on the aeroplane, she didn't want to waste a moment.

"We have to be a little careful. We can't alert them just yet to the fact that we are searching for her. If they understand that they may simply lock her away. The very fact that you are English might warn them off if they hear we are searching.

"But one thing we can do is follow up your contacts from Sheffield. I think we can ask them for help without the gangs getting to know. Do you have the details to hand?"

"Sure." Alana pulled out her phone and scrolled down to the names, addresses and phone numbers that Sheila Mitchell had dictated to her in Sheffield the previous Sunday evening. "Here they are. Maybe you call them, Jenni, and explain the situation?"

Jenni showed the details to Sophie who nodded firmly and said, "Vraiment, C'est las meme organisation que j'ai vous recommender."

So she punched in the number, and her call was answered immediately. "Mention our Sheffield friend, Sheila Mitchell," whispered Steph, and so Jenni did, as she introduced herself and explained their quest. The reply from the other end seemed very friendly and positive, and they could see Jenni was agreeing to meet up with the person on the line, "a bientôt".

"Marie-Krystina, the head of their group, is free to meet us today, and she doesn't work so very far from here. She suggests we go across town to their office now, and give her a better description of Leontine. I can use the same photos on my phone of her in a group of schoolgirls I sent through to you on Christmas day. It may help."

Sophie told them to leave their cases in her care, and to return for dinner with her. She'd call her police contacts, and find out as much as she could, but she said she expected Marie-Krystina would have even more reliable knowledge. She assured them she hoped they would return to stay the night with her when they had visited the other agency.

Sophie seemed anxious to make them as welcome as possible, saying it was not by choice that she lived alone, and she welcomed company over the next few days. Steph and

Alana beamed at her, very happy to stay in a cosy apartment, rather than a chilly and anonymous hotel. Clearly she and Jenni would have a lot of catching up to do about their years in West Africa together, anyway.

After a coffee with Sophie, the three set out once more and, unencumbered with any luggage walked briskly back to the Metro station and took the train to another working-class area of Brussels. They then needed to jump on a tram as well for two stops, so Steph was especially grateful to have Jenni with them.

The trams were still crowded in the middle hours of the day, with everyone still enjoying the post-Christmas chance to grab bargains in the city-centre sales, much the same as in London. The number of people in black padded jackets and dark trousers far exceeded any others. Black was the new black, it seemed.

Steph couldn't understand it, the propensity for Europeans to all want to dress so drearily, and in such sombre tones. The lovely flowing cottons and bright colours which would enliven an African street scene, and the brilliant silks of Asia were nowhere to be seen. It was as though the whole of Western society was in mourning, despite the public holidays. Only the light displays everywhere on the main streets dispelled the gloom of winter.

A Girl on the Plane

Chapter 19

Sisters of Ferocity.

Jenni seemed to know where she was going, either that, or she had exceptionally good instincts for orienteering, and within the hour they were knocking on a street door not so different from the one into Sophie's apartment building. But this wasn't a domestic address. They had entered a block of old, early 20th century offices, with worn wooden stairs and a pervading smell of damp floor mops and cheap disinfectant.

There was the welcome sight of a lift, however, which had a rather insecure gate as its only barrier, and it winched them six flights up to the attic offices of the agency. A woman who was obviously Marie Krystina came out to meet them as she heard the lift ascending.

She shook hands, and said, "Bonjour, the friends of Sheila, and of Sophie! Sheila emailed me to say you might be coming, and to look out for any word of your young girl. I think I may have something of interest for you."

"You have? That would be wonderful," said Alana. "We are flying on a wing and a prayer here, trying to find one child in a city of 1.5 million people."

"Come through into my office, and I'll tell you what I've heard."

Marie-Krystina was dressed in the black jeans and sweater uniform Steph had just observed on the streets, but her bobbed hair was coloured a bright golden-red, which almost shone in the December gloom, and she had a sharp, intelligent quickness about her, which Steph appreciated. They followed her back into a small, overcrowded office, with three desks all with computers and piles of brown paper files. But she was alone in the workspace today.

"Take a chair each, please. My colleagues won't return until next week. I just came in today to try to tackle the end of year financial reckoning. We can't afford an accountant or book-keeper, so it's part of my job description."

Steph said, "Sorry to ask something we should already know, but what do you do here exactly?"

"It's not very exact, but we rescue trafficked girls, and try to influence the policy makers of Europe to crack down on the gangs who exploit them."

When she spoke, it was with a light Polish accent, and her English had been learned there, rather than in Belgium.

"Yes, as you might guess, I myself am a graduate of the University of the Streets. Although I escaped before anything too bad happened to me. We are based in Brussels, because it is a civilized place to work and it puts us close to the European Parliament, but the problem is universal. We could just as well set up in Berlin, or Paris or Amsterdam, or even London."

Jenni was impatient for news. "So, can you tell us about our poor Leontine?"

"I have a contact who tells me a new group of girls has been delivered to a house we are watching in the suburbs, just last weekend. They are mainly Albanian and Bulgarian we believe, but there is definitely at least one African girl with them, possibly two.

"We have a reliable informer who lives in a house opposite and he saw them arrive late last week, Thursday or maybe Friday. It was dusk, so he couldn't see any faces clearly. But his information is usually to be believed. In fact, this is the news we have been hoping for, for some time. A fresh group of young women we can rescue before they are beaten, drugged and raped until they are too terrified to escape."

"Our friend Sophie, where we have just been, says she has a link in the vice squad in the police. Do you know people there as well?"

"Yeah, I know Sophie. Her agency concentrates more on asylum seekers who give up hope and are therefore easy prey for these gang-masters. But we work with the same Brussels police department. Once I have verified the information, I'm going to ask the police to help us raid the house and see who is inside. With good fortune, your girl will be there."

"Have you ever heard of a Portuguese-Angolan guy called Sonny Alvares?" asked Jenni. "We think he might have been the man who Steph here saw on the flight over, sitting next to Leontine. I know him from the DRC, a seriously nasty little piece of shit."

Alana blinked as she heard the epithet fall so easily from Sister Jenni's mouth. Nuns had widened their vocabulary from her school days! But Marie-Krystina endorsed the description.

"Oh yes, that low-life! If he is in the location I'm thinking of, then it would be an added bonus if we can get him arrested. He acts as one of the couriers in and out of Africa."

"Marie-Krystina, how far from here is it?" asked Steph, all set to run over and barge into the house that very afternoon.

The red-headed woman replied, "Call me Marie. Marie-Krystina is such a mouthful. About ten kilometres on the road north towards Antwerp. There's a great corridor of similar places from Tangiers northwards all the way to Stockholm and through the Baltic countries. We are trying to establish safe houses, like refuges, to match each one, where girls can find help."

"A British parliamentary report described the sex trade in the UK as exploitation on an industrial scale," said Alana.

"That's right," said Marie. "And our resources to combat it are very small. But in Belgium there are some good officers in the police. They are on our side, and people we can trust not to warn them when a raid is planned. That happens more often than you would believe. All it takes is a few thousand euros and a blind eye to turn, and then when the houses are raided, there are no girls to be found, and no evidence of any brothel business or prostitution. They are clever, these devils."

"So, what now?"

"Make yourselves comfortable. Brew some tea if you like. I am going to call my associate, and then bring this to the attention of the police department. We will have to take our lead from them, about how to approach the property. The men in charge, or women, (because there are also women who exploit these girls,) may well be armed and dangerous. They don't hesitate to kill if they think their profits are under attack. It happened to the partner of a very good friend of mine a few years ago a documentary film-maker who had the evidence to expose them."

"You don't mean Carrie, Bel's girlfriend?"

"Yes! How do you know Bel?"

"She's my boss!" shouted Steph. "This is unreal. Everyone I meet, including Jenni here, seems to know Bel. How are you and her friends?!"

Marie replied, "Oh, Bel and I go back to the 2000s when we were both in our twenties. We were on a pan-European campaigning group together. But I haven't seen her for ages, not since before the dreadful news about Carrie. They had the funeral in Italy, where Carrie's parents lived and it was too difficult for me to get there. How is Bel these days?"

"She nearly died earlier this year in a horrible road-accident but was brought back to recovery by a young medic. And they are now on their honeymoon! It ended like a romantic fairy-tale."

"Mon Dieu! You must tell me more when we have time. And you two? Are you together, or am I imagining a relationship?"

Steph pulled a little face and reached over to give Alana a little hug. "No, you don't imagine anything. We have been together for three years. Ally here is my soul-mate, and much else besides. She's brilliant with numbers, and is one of the best forensic accountants in the UK."

Alana squirmed slightly, and said nothing, either to agree or deny Steph's description. She changed the subject back to their immediate business.

"OK, shall I make tea, while you call your contacts? Then we maybe should think about returning to Sophie's place for the night. We can go to spring Leontine from her trap tomorrow morning? It sounds a good plan."

So Ally made the tea, which they all drank without milk, as is normal on the continent, and the hot liquid curled its way into Steph's cold stomach and gave her confidence that this elusive chase would have a positive resolution. Marie-Krystina spoke some time on the telephone, to one person, and then re-dialled to talk to someone else. When she put the phone down she looked very satisfied.

"Well, it's on. Very early tomorrow. We've been told to keep well clear, but they are sending a team of armed officers to the house. They trust our intelligence."

"But I must be there to identify Leontine and rescue her if she is one of the girls. She will be terrified otherwise." Jenni didn't trust any police not to traumatize her fostered daughter. But Marie reassured her.

"I know the officers in the vice squad. They are mainly female, and very experienced in this sort of case. We'll be told where they are taking any girls they find, and we can go to join them there. The raid will be before dawn, so it will be very difficult for you to find the place anyway."

She continued, "I suggest we all go home now and get some sleep. I will accompany you back to the Metro station if you like. My head is too worn out to cope with these books any more, anyway. The longer I stay in the spreadsheets, the more mess I seem to make."

"If you need help, I can give you a hand for the next day or two," volunteered Alana, surprising herself, as well as the others. "It's what I do."

Marie-Krystina looked astonished, and then a broad grin spread across her features. "Could you? Even if you could only spare me an hour or two to check through my formulae, and show me where I'm going wrong, I would be so grateful. I have to file these accounts by the year end, and no way are they fit to go right now."

"Let's wait until after we get Leontine back, obviously, but then, sure. I can spend Sunday and Monday with you. I'd be happy to."

Steph looked at the smiles shared between Alana and the undeniably attractive Polish woman, and felt a sharp prick of what she had to admit was old-fashioned jealousy. Alana's gifts were so far from her own comfort-zone, that maybe she didn't offer her enough positive feedback. Mostly she simply teased Ally about her "really boring" profession. She suddenly thought they should close down the session and leave, as had been suggested.

Everyone bundled themselves back into their winter coats or jackets, and Marie locked up the top-floor office.

"The lift only takes three at a time. You go on and I'll run down the stairs. It's part of my fitness regime."

She bustled them all into the tiny box, and closed the gate for them. "I'll race you to the bottom!" she laughed, and then as they descended at a stately pace, they could see and hear her running down the stairs beside them. They made it to the ground floor in front of her, but only by a second or two.

"I couldn't do that going up," she laughed, as they tumbled out. Then she led them out of the building back onto the city streets, which were already dark with the fading light, and full of the noise and bustle of jostling rush-hour traffic.

Friday night in Brussels came to meet them as they jumped onto a tram and returned to the local metro station. Marie-Krystina took another line and bade them farewell, but she said she'd call first thing to Jenni's phone, as soon as she had news about Leontine. Jenni who had become rather quiet, probably due to deepening angst about her little ward, nodded gratefully and said, "We'll be waiting, don't worry. And if it takes funds to get her to safety, I do have sufficient money, don't worry."

It was past seven when they made it back to Sophie's place, and by then Alana and Steph both had aching feet and felt they'd had a whistle-stop tour of central Brussels.

"We must come again sometime, when we're not so focused on a mission. I'm sure there are lots to see, and the by-words for Belgium are beer and chocolate after all. It can't be bad," said Alana.

"Let's take a large box of truffles home for Bel and Bryony. I missed the wedding so I owe them a nice present," said Steph. She was thinking again how much she missed Isabel, not having her at hand to give her continual endorsement and words of wisdom.

She still had a professional crush on Isabel, from the first day she had been interviewed by her for the post at Righteous Anger, and her admiration for the boss had never weakened. To hear so many people speak so highly of her over the last week or so, strengthened the feeling.

As soon as they were home in London, she decided she would consult Bel privately about what Alana had asked her to do, to pass it by her and get her feedback. Jenni's joining their household yesterday had pushed out the issues of commitment and the B word from their conversations temporarily, but she knew it hadn't gone away, any more than Ally's suppressed tension on the matter would suddenly relax, and let Steph off the hook permanently.

The long climb up sixty stone steps to Sophie's apartment was rewarded by a delicious smell of something wonderful cooking as she opened the door.

"It's boeuf-en-bier," Sophie said. "I hope you like it, how do you call it in English, old-fashioned stew?"

"It's what we in Lancashire call hot-pot, and the Liverpudlians call 'Scouse'," laughed Alana, "And look, we picked these up on the way. Deux petits cadeaux pour toi," and she handed over one of the two large boxes of Belgian chocolates they had bought in the shopping centre opposite the last Metro station. Sophie looked very happy, as expected, as Alana had guessed correctly that a sudden surprise of a box of chocolates, even in Belgium, would rarely fail to please.

The warmth of the small apartment, after Sophie drew the window curtains against the dark city night, helped them all to relax and eased the tensions of the day. Simple friendship, good food and kind hospitality settled their nerves, and when they went to bed, the three visitors sharing a family room together, everyone expected good news the following day. Steph and Ally shared the double bed and Jenni took the cot in the corner. They heard her quietly praying in the darkness for the safety of her young charge.

A Girl on the Plane

Chapter 20

A spoke in the wheel.

Unfortunately, the next morning things didn't exactly go to plan. Ally woke as usual on the dot of 6 am, but with the added hour on the continent, she realized it was already 7 am in Belgium, and she could hear Sophie in the kitchen pottering about making coffee or preparing a breakfast table for the visitors. She left the other two women fast asleep, with Jenni no doubt still recovering from jet-lag, pulled on her robe and slippers and padded out to join their host.

"No news yet?" she asked as she wondered if Sophie had heard anything from Marie.

" Non, je regrette. Café? The´?"

"Café, s'il vous plait."

She took the offered cup and sipped it appreciatively. Sophie had turned on the national TV station which was playing a weather forecast, and they watched it together. Outside, the cold gloom had turned into a Saturday of persistent rain. Allie could hear it pouring down against the roof above their heads and also lashing against the windows.

Would that make it a good day or a bad one for a police raid on a traffickers' den?

Sophie had obviously nipped out earlier to a nearby boulangerie and bought a bag of freshly baked croissants, which were warming in the small oven of her gas cooker. Allie carried her coffee with her into the bathroom, and decided to take a quick shower while she was there. There were several clean towels set ready, and she took the top one from the pile.

The shower revived her even more than the coffee and she felt strong and competent to deal with whatever the day would throw at them. When she returned to the kitchen, showered and dressed again in her pyjamas and gown, the other two had also emerged from the bedroom and Jenni was talking rapidly to Sophie about something. Ally slipped past them and went to dress, and Stephanie followed her back into the bedroom.

"I think we may have a little bit of a situation to deal with, if they don't find Leontine unharmed. Jenni is getting seriously stressed," she whispered.

"What do you mean, honey?"

"Didn't you hear her in the night? She was having nightmares and thrashed about shouting and crying out more than once. I'm surprised she didn't wake us both up."

"No, I slept through, dead to the world."

"How do you think we should play it? Should I tell her she was talking in her sleep?"

"No, it will only stress her more. Let her sub-conscious mind take care of itself. But I think we should dress and be ready to move as soon as we get a call."

Steph nodded and decided to follow Ally's lead and make a quick visit to the bathroom. Within fifteen minutes they were both sitting fully dressed at Sophie's table, sampling the local croissants. Huge, air-filled, so buttery and warm to the touch and to the mouth, they were completely delicious.

Some traditions, like continental breakfasts, were best left pure and unsullied. The coffees were served in deep wide cups, rather like bowls, and for a few minutes, both women felt they were on holiday in some delightful pent-house Airbnb.

Jenni, who had dressed but hadn't bothered to shower, was still on the call from Marie, which had come in while Steph was in the shower. When she came off the line, she looked sombre.

"Marie-Krystina has been bringing me up to speed with developments. The police vice squad raided the house. That part went well, and they've arrested three men and a woman. Six trafficked girls were found there, and are now in protective custody, while their identities are checked.

"But for us, it was a disaster. Sonny Alvarez had staying been there until yesterday morning, but then he left, taking the two African girls with him. One of the other men started to break ranks with the rest, and divulged this information. They are all in the hands of the police right now, and they are trying to get some more addresses and information from him and the others."

"Damn!" swore Steph, "If we'd been a day or two earlier this wouldn't have happened, and now we're back to square one."

"Not really," said Alana, ever the voice of reason. "Jenni only arrived in London on Thursday, and we came as quickly as we could. We now know who Leontine is, and that she was in that house until early yesterday. The net's closing in."

"But where are they now, and how do we get to them?" asked Steph.

"Marie-Krystina is going to call me back as soon as she has something definite to tell us. But whatever we hear, she suggests we return to her office. I think she also has hopes that Alana will help her complete the end of year accounts there."

Jenni joined them at the kitchen table, and they shared out the rest of the croissants. Sophie made another large cafetiere of coffee and they took that as well. The news that they had nearly managed to reach Leontine, but had missed her by twenty-four hours, in what only God knew were perilous circumstances, depressed them all. And their mood wasn't helped by the rain which still pelted down unceasingly past the windows.

Eventually there was nothing left on the table to eat, and they pushed back their chairs with a comfortable groan, all thanking Sophie for her simple but delicious breakfast.

"Come on, let's hit the streets. We can't sit here all day taking up Sophie's time."

But Sophie obviously enjoyed their company. In fact, she suggested she went with them round to the other agency. It was Saturday, nothing else to do, and she was as worried about Jenni's young charge as the rest of them. So that was how a party of four women ventured out into the rain under a couple of Sophie's umbrellas and made the journey across the city to 'Les Soeurs.'

Sophie knew a different route which involved less walking and a longer tram ride. It gave them more of an over-ground view of the city, and also cut ten minutes off the journey. When they reached the office building, and were about to take the rickety lift up the stairs, Steph gallantly agreed to do the walking instead of overcrowding the tiny box.

"Remember? Three people maximum, I'm the youngest, and anyway, when you get to the top I'll call it down and maybe take a ride for the last couple of floors."

So she waved them up and then started to jog up the stairs. She was naturally fit and liked to keep that way, but by the third floor her lungs were burning. She heard the lift doors open and shut above her, and rang the bell to call it. Maybe she wasn't so fit after all, as the ride up the last couple of floors did feel good.

When she joined the others in the office, she saw that Marie-Krystina wasn't alone. There were two police female officers with her, from the vice squad, and they were asking to see her files of suspected traffickers. Sophie immediately joined in what was clearly quite a heated conversation. All four people seemed to know each other and be on first names terms.

"These officers," explained Marie, "they need me to corroborate their identification of the men and the women they arrested this morning, even though they have the whole of Interpol at their disposal. We have gone through this so many times before, it tires me." She was showing them a ring-binder with more than fifty pages of faces and names.

"So many people involved? How can you stop them all?" Alana was shocked by how thick and full the ring-binder was.

"These are from all over Europe and the file covers what we knew of them over the last five years. Carrie Monterini helped me compile it, and I would bet 1000 euros that somewhere in these pages we will find the face of the man who killed her. I have another folder full of images of the trafficked victims."

The police were cross-referencing with a group of faces they had on their phones, mug-shots they had only taken that morning. It was clear they had suspected the people they'd arrested had all given false names.

Jenni produced her own picture from her phone. "This is the girl we are searching for," she said in French to the police officers, a man and a woman. "It is essential we locate her today. Her life could be in great danger."

The words *life* and *danger* seemed to concentrate their

minds, and they were more forthcoming about the raid they'd conducted and what information they had. It was more than they'd previously told Marie. When they had finished, Jenni said to the English women, "Did you understand any of that?"

"They mentioned something about Antwerp?"

"Yes, they think that is where Alvarez took the girls. The port has a thriving sex –trade and he may have thought to "break them in" up there first."

Sophie and Marie then both said the same thing. "L'hotel des quatre vents!" Sophie explained, "The Four Winds Hotel. It's a location we have both been suspicious about, a sort of holding centre for asylum seekers, but it also has a very bad reputation as a sort of slave auction centre for sex workers. It is on the outskirts of Antwerp, and we have been asking the police to close it down for months."

Marie-Krystina added, "This information must have come out under interrogation since I spoke to you earlier. We know where it is. I don't think this time we can afford to simply leave it to the police. We must go ourselves."

The police, who understood English, both shook their heads in alarm and told her not to be so foolish, but all three of the French speakers turned on them together, and said again that lives were at stake. Would they contact their Antwerp colleagues and ask them to meet with them at the address later this morning, because if not, then they would definitely all go without support? Steph chimed in on behalf of her and Alana as well and concurred. They would all go!

Faced with five assertive women, the police hastily agreed it was a priority to track down Alvarez and the girls he had with him, and if they thought the address near Antwerp was a definite possibility then they would set up a link to Antwerp and get all the officers and vehicles they could muster to wait for them nearby.

"But how can we get transport? How far is it?"

"Only 45 kilometres on the A12. It'll take less than forty minutes."

"Then we can hire a taxi!" said Jenni.

"No need," said Marie-Krystina. "I have my car with me

this morning. It's parked round the back. But it's small, only a Fiat. It will only take three passengers and if we need to bring Leontine back in it as well…"

Alana saw the problem. "Don't worry, you take Steph and Jenni maybe, with you, and Sophie and I will stay here and get started on those accounts."

Sophie seemed happy with that arrangement. She was heavy and elderly after all, and not the type to be much use in a surprise raid and rescue operation. The police started to take down details of the migrant centre address and then called their colleagues in Antwerp to request co-operation.

Marie-Krystina pulled out a chair in front of her desk top computer for Alana and opened the screen with her pin number which she wrote down on the pad.

"If you can sort me out with the finances, you are an angel," she said. "I will love you forever."

Alana opened her spectacle case and pulled out her glasses, perching them on her nose. Even Steph wanted to kiss her there and then, she looked so adorable, and Marie-Krystina was virtually salivating in appreciation.

"They aren't complicated accounts. We sadly don't have sufficient income to make it a massive task, but I must balance the books, and I'm sure I have really messed up the formulas and think they are in the wrong columns. Here. Let me show you a copy of last year's accounts for comparison", and she switched to another workbook.

Alana entered the screen into the enchanted world of her natural environment, and enjoyed the prospect of stalking through the spreadsheet undergrowth in search of errors.

"Leave it with me. It will take my mind off all the danger you are walking yourselves into. Just call me, Steph. Don't leave me in the dark!"

"Of course. I promise."

"I'll make sure she doesn't," said Jenni, and then they and the police were all out of the door and Alana and Sophie were alone. Sophie looked at Alana, happy at the computer, and did what she was so good at, making them both some coffee.

Chapter 21

Rescued!

The motorway from Brussels northwards to Antwerp was a major route up through Europe and was packed with trucks and container lorries heading for the giant port, even on the Saturday after Christmas. Steph let Jenni sit in the front of the car, so she could talk easily to Marie-Krystina, while she bent her long legs under her and tried to calm her nerves in the back seat.

The spray from the passing traffic added to the rain still pouring down, and affected their visibility badly, and their three sets of breathed out carbon dioxide made the windows in the little Fiat Panda steam up. Marie turned the heater up as high as it would go, and the wipers flicked back and forth with a rapid swish-swish.

Steph didn't see how their encounter with the Alvarez guy, and any other cronies he might have, would be anything other than violent, For this reason, she was so grateful for Ally's quiet preference for back-room work. She couldn't bear the thought that she might be hurt. This wasn't a game. The people they were dealing with were seriously dangerous. The ghost of poor Carrie Monterini bore witness to that.

The address where they were heading was halfway round the circular "Ring", the highly congested orbital route round the city of Antwerp, but it seemed no time at all before Marie was turning left and then right under the motorway and off into a semi-industrial suburb, full of cheap cafes and what looked like warehousing.

A few more turns and then she pulled up the car. Steph could see a row of three police vehicles up ahead on a side street, and breathed a small sigh of relief. She wasn't a wimp, but official back-up might prevent the encounter getting very nasty, very quickly.

Marie had obviously known exactly where her police liaison officers would be. Leaving the other two inside, she leaped out of the car and ran through the rain to talk to the four men in the first patrol car. Jenni, though, wasn't going to be side-lined and jumped out on the right hand side, so Steph, pushed the front seat forward and ducked out after her.

The police began to leave their vehicles and looked less than thrilled to see them, but Marie said, about |Jenni and Stephanie, "It's essential they are with us. They can identify the girl we are searching for."

The four burly men were armed and dressed with protective chest and back vests, gloves, boots and an array of head gear. Steph felt rather under-dressed, but she was determined to see this through to the end.

The first police officer gave some stern instructions to Marie, but he spoke in Flemish, which Steph couldn't understand. Marie translated, "The hostel is just round the corner. He is telling us to stay well back. That's an order. They will go in and bring everyone out. Some of them will go round to the back to prevent people running away in that direction. They have brought a full squad of officers as they expect to arrest everyone in the building. There may be a whole company of illegal immigrants in there, which is sadly, why I think the police were so willing to co-operate with our rescue mission for your girl."

So, against their will, Steph and Jenni walked quietly round the corner and then stayed well back, while Marie-Krystina edged just a little closer. They all had a clear view of the nondescript grey-clad building which looked just like a run-down truckers' inn. The police pulled down the visors over their faces and made a concerted run at the main entrance, and as they shouted their arrival, it was obvious that pandemonium was breaking out inside. Steph had only witnessed such scenes on TV cop shows, but the reality was every bit as rough and noisy as the fictional dramas.

She could hear screams and shouts and people running back and forth, but thankfully no sound of gun-shots. It was over in less than ten minutes, though it felt like ages. But more than a dozen men came out first, their hands in the air, and their heads bowed and trying to avoid recognition from the video camera one of the police officers was using to film the arrests. They were quickly cuffed, and led away to the big police closed van.

"Is he among them?" hissed Steph to Jenni. "I don't see him."

"No, neither do I. I hope we've got the right location," she whispered back.

But then a second wave of residents emerged, two bewildered families with several small children, and then finally, Sonny Alvarez himself, in handcuffs struggling and swearing and generally hurling insults at the police.

But where were the kidnapped girls? Steph began to fear the worst, until one of the police officers came across to the women and said to them in French, "Can you come inside? I think we've found what you are searching for. But they are too traumatized to understand what we are telling them. I think it will be better if you come and help them realize they've been rescued."

They all needed no further prompting and ran past the police and remaining arrestees, into the building. The police who had fetched them took them into a back room which had been padlocked from the outside, and the police had broken the lock to open the door.

It was very dark, as the blinds had been drawn down on both its windows, and it didn't smell so good. There was a dirty mattress in the corner, and cowering against the wall, on it were two young African girls, their hands and feet still bound up with duck-tape. There was an unmistakable smell of urine. The police had removed their gags, but they were both whimpering like trapped creatures and looked petrified.

Marie quickly pulled up the blinds and unlocked the windows for good measure to let in a little fresh air. Jenni and Steph went forward to the youngsters and with help from a policeman and his pocket knife, freed their hands and feet from the tape.

Jenni was speaking in soothing tones in French and then in Lingala, "Leontine, don't be afraid. You are safe now, quite safe. We have come to rescue you. You are in safe hands now. We have come with the police. Nothing bad will happen to you now."

Steph knew, as well as she could know anything, that the older of the two girls, the one with a livid bruise across her face and a black eye, was definitely Leontine. She wanted to cry with relief, especially when she saw Jenni scoop her up in her arms and rock her like a baby. The girl had stopped whimpering but now was simply weeping profoundly, with shock, with relief, with love for the woman who had come so far to rescue her.

Steph thought she would be best employed doing much the same for the other captured girl. She wasn't from the Congo, and spoke English, although her voice was so quiet she was virtually inaudible, Steph gave her an old-fashioned hug, which was as well, because just then the police told them both not to touch the girls any more, talking about contaminating evidence. A new van of police officers had just turned up, this time with female officers who engaged Marie and Jenni in a long conversation about due process, and interviews and medical examinations.

Jenni said bluntly, "OK, we get your point. But we are accompanying these children at all times, and they are never leaving our sight."

The girls clung to the women as though their lives depended on it. They had been tied up for at least twenty-four hours, and were both totally inadequately dressed for mid-winter in Belgium. The police officers produced emergency blankets made of foil. Wrapped up in these, the girls were helped to their feet, and out of their nasty prison.

A vehicle looking rather like an ambulance drew up in front of the hostel, and Jenni, Steph and the girls were helped inside. Marie said, "You two stay with them. They are taking them to a special suite in the local hospital. It's for rape victims, just to warn you. We will be able to find out exactly what has happened to them. I will drive behind you in my car. This is a good result. They are alive, that's the main thing." And she waved at them all with a smile as the doors closed.

The next hours weren't easy, not for Jenni and Steph as they had to witness the trauma of the poor young victims of the trafficking and kidnapping, and certainly not for the girls themselves. Jenni acted as translator and mediator for them both, and the second girl was identified as an even younger fourteen-year-old high-school student from a region in northern Nigeria, who had endured a hellish journey across the Sahara and had been separated from her parents in Morocco. She had been bodily attacked and kidnapped along with a small group of other girls, and sent from Tangiers to Spain pushed behind a partition in the back of a truck.

Compared to her, Leontine, beaten and bruised as she was, had come off better, only fighting off Sonny Alvarez' horrible attentions for eight days. She was beaten up, because she had fought him like a cat at every turn. But both girls had been half starved, to sap their spirits and were both desperately thirsty and hungry when they reached the hospital.

At the hospital, the medical and counselling staff were both experienced and very kind, and made the necessary physical gathering of evidence of ill-treatment, the photographs of their injuries and the beatings across their back and legs, the internal examination and the taking of samples of blood and vaginal fluids as least traumatic as they could make it.

The girls still wept throughout, but once they were given hot sweet drinks and some soft sandwiches, they began to recover and stopped shaking so much. Leontine gripped Jenni's hand so tightly she made her knuckles go white, but she also obviously recognised Steph from the aeroplane and gave her a small, exhausted smile. "Merci, merci…" she mouthed.

The girls were then allowed to go and bathe, not just shower, but sink into deep old-fashioned bath-tubs of hot soapy water, which must have felt wonderful after what they'd been through. The hospital staff found them some soft pyjamas, and they were put to bed in adjoining bays, in a private ward.

Jenni settled down in an arm-chair next to Leontine's bed and prepared to hold a vigil. Steph was alarmed though, to see a policeman as well, standing guard outside their bay.

Marie explained, "They could be material witnesses in a very serious trafficking investigation. I've been told this is the breakthrough the Police Unit have been waiting for, for months. Thanks to your quick reactions, and Jenni's determination, we might have helped crack a case involving an international network of gangs and drug lords. So the police need to make sure these girls are safe."

Then Jenni said to Steph, "Don't forget to call Alana. She'll be very anxious to know how this all went."

Steph looked at her watch and saw that it was already well past mid-day. She groaned in self-reproach and hastily pulled out her phone to contact Alana.

"Not dead and buried in concrete under a flyover then?" was the laconic answer to her call. Ally was using her finest, "See if I care" voice, so Steph knew she was in deep trouble. Alana must have been waiting for news, good or bad for ages, but had been too proud to text and nudge her for an answer.

"No, all alive and we have Leontine. We are now in the hospital and I couldn't call before. I am so sorry, honey. But it's been non-stop here. There was a police raid, which went according to plan, and then we found Leontine and another girl imprisoned in a darkened room at the back of the hotel. We've come with them here for them to be debriefed and looked after and I think they will be kept in hospital under observation for at least twenty-four hours. Jenni will stay here, but I think Marie and I are returning to you and Sophie very soon."

"Stay as long as you need to. We are fine here. Well, I am still re-doing these end of year accounts, but Sophie has gone shopping to buy food for our evening meal. Marie really is a hopeless book-keeper by the way. Don't tell her I said so, though."

"Well she did warn you, and say that she was desperate for your help. You're her good angel, and we have all been crucial in rescuing poor Leontine. I think we can be justifiably proud about our trip over here."

"How is she?"

"Battered, bruised and initially traumatised. The girls had been beaten and starved as well as tied up. But her spirit will come back. One good thing is that the medics don't believe either of them have been raped or sexually assaulted yet. They were being kept as trophies for later. I'll tell you more when I see you."

Steph could almost hear Ally's deep sigh of relief and caught the release of tension evident in her next words. "You are all safe, that's the main thing. And I am happy I've had these accounts to correct. I can't imagine how I would have felt just waiting to hear, without anything to take my mind off what you were facing up in Antwerp. I love you, darling."

"And I love you too. We'll be home for supper. Don't worry."

Once both the girls were tucked up in bed, they quickly fell asleep as natural exhaustion took precedence over anything else. Jenni confirmed what Stephanie had expected her to say. She would stay on with them in the hospital for as long as it took. Marie and Steph were to return to Brussels and she would liaise with them and with the police as necessary the following day.

"I'm perfectly happy. I'm where I need to be."

"Well, if you're sure," said Marie-Krystina, "I need to go home, to cook tea. My kids are returning from their father's tonight, and I have to be there for them."

"You have children?" asked Steph later as she sat next to Marie for the ride back to Brussels. Somehow it was a side of the woman she had never imagined before.

"Oh yes, my three monsters, but I adore them all. Husbands may come and go, but children are forever. I have two boys and a girl."

And for the rest of the trip she talked to Steph all about her family, how she had married and divorced within ten years, and her children were now ten, eight and six years old. They had spent Christmas with their father, a civil rights lawyer she'd met through her work, and he was a good dad, just better at short visits and weekend stays than the daily grind of school- work supervision, mountains of laundry, and understanding all the ups and downs of being a child in 2019.

Then she tossed a hard ball straight at Stephanie. "You, and the beautiful Alana, have you considered children? It is so easy today, and you would make lovely parents."

Stephanie went hot as she could feel her colour change. "Um, well, we have discussed it, but with my job I need to travel so much, I can't see it working out. Anyway, we're not even married."

Marie looked at her sideways, with a raised eyebrow expression, as if she found that answer pretty lame. "So? Is it a commitment thing? Are you not sure about Alana? You don't need a piece of paper. If she was my partner . . ."

"Well she's not, she's mine!" Steph almost snapped at her, alarmed how direct and personal Marie was being.

"O.K! I respect that. Don't worry. Just saying though..."

"What?"

"She's a beautiful, clever and unselfish woman, and I can tell she's unhappy. Maybe that's something you can fix. But don't let me interfere in your marriage."

"Like I said, we're not married!"

"Well, so you say. What do I know anyway? It's just that I regret letting my marriage go so easily. I just didn't prioritize it enough, neither of us did. And I can see what you two have, it is special. I am very envious. If you love her, and she loves you, then don't let it slip away from you. And like I said, I think you'd both make wonderful lesbian mothers!"

Steph was thoroughly churned up by this impromptu therapy session from the very direct and thoroughly annoying Polish woman sitting beside her. She sank into a not-quite-sullen silence, cross that Marie was so perceptive, but they entered the streets of Brussels and returned to Marie's office almost before she knew it, and the conversation ended with the journey.

Chapter 22

An answer to her prayers.

By the time they parked the car and walked round to the office, the heavy rain clouds had moved north and the Brussels streets were gleaming wet, but the air was still and smelled fresh and clean. No need to run up the stairs with only two of them, so they came through the door as smoothly as if they were on skates, and Stephanie didn't have to bend over a desk gasping for breath. It was almost dark though, and the lights were on.

"How did you get on, Ally?" asked Marie, a little nervously, but with the tone of someone hoping for good news.

"All done, my friend. Your end-of-year accounts can be submitted on Monday with a clear conscience, but I would like an hour with you before you click 'Send', to explain what I've done, and why I've done it. I've also set you up a new workbook complete with formulae which will make next year's books much easier to keep straight."

"You are an answer to my prayers, an angel!" laughed Marie. "I could kiss you!"

"Hey, none of that!" objected Stephanie, only half joking.

"Well, I have to run now, to get home before my children, but maybe on Monday evening, how about we all go out to celebrate? And I hope you can stay over to see the New Year in with us as well. Leontine will be in hospital under observation for a day or too yet, I'm sure."

"But our job is done here," said Steph. "We've helped Jenni reunite with her, and we can't impose on Sophie's kindness much longer."

Alana disagreed though. "Sophie and I have been having a long bi-lingual chat, and she tells me she wants to be our tour guide and show us the sights of Brussels before we leave. She says there is so much to see. Neither of us is expected back at work until Thursday, so if it's OK with you, I would love to stay for a few more days."

Steph pulled a little face, but then smiled. Whatever Allie wanted to make her happy, that's what she wanted too. And if Jenni was camping out in Antwerp hospital overnight, then they would have Sophie's spare room to themselves. This was an encouraging thought.

Marie took her silence as agreement, and said, "Fantastic! Now I must run. Sorry I have to evict you both, but I have to lock up as I go. We are the only ones in the building, and the ground floor big door needs a double lock.

They gathered up their possessions and left alongside her. Sophie had made her own way home with freshly bought meat and vegetables for another gourmet meal an hour earlier, so Ally and Steph had to navigate the city by themselves. Steph pulled Alana towards her and linked their arms. Alana wound the last four feet of her scarf so it went round Steph's neck as well as her own, and they strode together through the bustle of the shoppers and festive revellers pouring out of every bar.

Their Saturday evening in Brussels was much less tense than the previous night had been, worrying about Leontine's fate, and what lay ahead. Sophie, who obviously loved cooking had produced a sweet casserole of pork and apple, laced with some calvados, a huge mound of buttery mashed potatoes, and some spiced red cabbage.

Ally and Steph did full justice to it, and afterwards they sat together in front of Sophie's electric fire and ate some wonderful truffles from the box they had given her. The longer she was in their company, the more Sophie remembered her 'crusty' English, and she shared many stories with them about her life teaching in Africa, and then the work she did with the refugee charity.

Steph didn't like to interrogate her about her age, but reckoned she must be well into her seventies.

"Have you any thoughts of retiring," she asked.

"What have I got facing me if I do?" replied Sophie. "I have no children. That is my biggest regret. When I was young I was very, how you say, driven, focussed on my work. I thought family life was not necessary. Now, I wish I had made space for it. I had offers, you know, good offers! One local chief in Cameroon wanted me to be his fourth wife!"

"I hope you sent him packing!" laughed Alana.

"Yes, certainly. But here in Belgium, I had several possibilities. I just chose another path. I must live with my decisions."

She sounded subdued and not as happy as she had been before. Steph wanted to break the mood away from the sadness of childlessness, which she guessed Ally would be feeding on.

"I see you have some mint tea on the shelf. Can I make us all a cup before we go to bed?" The others nodded, and she went into Sophie's little kitchen to boil the water.

Unlike the previous night, when they had hardly touched each other in the double bed, very shy in front of Jenni lying only three feet away from them in the cot, this time, as they un-dressed, it was obvious to both of them that they were going to have sex, at least a nice long session of making out, but possibly further down the road to full-on orgasmic rapture,. They kept their pyjamas on for deccncy's sake, but as soon as they heard Sophie's bedroom door close, Steph was on to Ally curled in the bed beside her.

What she couldn't express successfully in words, she wanted to show by her actions. She rolled towards her beautiful partner and started by brushing the fringe of hair delicately back from her forehead before taking her chin between her fingers and bringing their mouths together. She ran her tongue over Alana's teeth and then invaded her mouth with hers, flicking her tongue deep inside and enjoying the sweet minty taste.

Alana felt so good, so soft and so firm at the same time, and she seemed as hungry as Steph was. Stephanie put her hands up and under Alana's soft pyjama top and felt the contours of her back, firm and strong. Good slim back. Alana's self-control and exercise routines had given her excellent muscle-tone and a neat figure. Constant attention to detail kept her fit.

"Up, darling!" murmured Steph, tugging at the cream

pajama top and Alana lifted her shoulders, so it could be pulled off over her head. Steph then set about kissing her breasts, one by one, and very delicately, sucking on each rosy nipple in turn, until Alana writhed on the bed and tossed under her.

Things heated up, and Steph's firm hands now disposed of the pyjama bottoms. She flipped them both over and pulled Ally on top of her so she could take the weight of her lover and feel her body against hers, from top to bottom.

She gripped Ally's neat little ass with one hand, and held her head so her mouth was captured, with the other. She knew she had learned from Ally how to make love to her in the way she liked, and she was almost complacent about it.

"Not… fair…" murmured Alana. "Let's get you naked as well." And soon both their nightclothes lay on the floor. Steph was taking the lead, and there was no hint of tiredness, jet-lag or anything else in her actions. She knew Ally liked it just a little bit rough, well maybe that wasn't the right word, more like "firm".

She always responded very well when Steph got directive. In the dark it was just their bodies talking to each other, and her body took over. She pulled Alana back on top of her, but this time facing upwards, so her body was open and exposed to her powerful hands, and she couldn't respond easily with her own initiative.

"Lie back on my shoulder, and keep quiet," Steph whispered, as she kept kissing Ally's sensitive sweet spot just behind her ear, but where her hands were going was somewhere even more sensitive.

Alana lay on top of Steph and tried to chill out, to relax and delay the inevitable rise in her libido. She knew the woman below her was appreciating the feel of her weight pressing down on her body. Her head rested against Steph's shoulder, but for the rest of her, she seemed to be melting into Steph's own body.

Steph had one hand still playing a game with her breasts, but her other hand was feeling its way down across her rib cage, over the plane of her belly, and then down between her legs. Then Steph lifted her own thigh between Alana's legs, so she was straddled over her, even more aroused, even less able to control what was going on.

Steph's right hand began to circle Ally's clit, very, very lightly, and as Ally started to buck against it, aching for something stronger something deeper, she felt Steph's leg between hers began to rise up and down. She could feel herself growing slippery and Steph's fingers then moved forward and easily penetrated her, while a wicked thumb kept pressure on her swollen clit.

Being held in this position was impossibly arousing, but also frustrating in the sense that she could do nothing herself, except ask and plead, aching for more, and hoping for a release into a climax. She was coming undone.

Steph was providing just enough pressure to arouse and provoke her, but not enough to push her over the fence into orgasm. She was making her wait yet again, as Ally had been forced to wait on so many previous occasions, and inside all the sexual fireworks between them, a little spark of anger stirred inside Alana's breast.

"More, more," she breathed, demanding Steph push harder, deeper.

But Steph seemed to be enjoying the torture, and took her time, assuming she could control the speed and the pace of their love-making, and Ally suddenly decided she couldn't bear to be so passive any longer.

She gave an almighty buck and pushed Steph's hands away from her. Then she turned in a flash, and took command of the whole situation. Now it was her mouth which invaded Steph's, now it was her hands which spread Steph's legs and forced them wide apart, her fingers which began to play her like a violin. Before long she had Steph sobbing and pleading for relief, which she gave her willingly.

Stephanie lay back panting. She suddenly seemed to have gone from dominant hunter, to a conquered and rather baffled prey. Alana knew she had surprised her, and was rather pleased with herself. In a tiny way, it had been payback for being made to wait hours for news earlier, for having to be the one who was done to, not the one who did, not the one who took the initiative.

Even after two plus years they were still learning about each other, and the fire inside Alana which she normally kept so firmly underground needed to be acknowledged. She needed to remind Stephanie, whom she adored, that it was always there, and needed to be released. If it wasn't, then she might just explode and take the wreckage of their relationship with her.

They didn't speak to each other again with words, just with caresses and then made a joint attempt to mop themselves up slightly. Steph pulled a box of tissues from the bed-side table and passed some over to Alana. She dropped kisses all across Alana's soft abdomen and the tops of her thighs, but she wasn't playing tricks or trying to provoke a second round.

Alana had made her point and she thought she understood inside, what her lover was saying. Alana had communicated something profound to her through her love-making, but it was also a subtle thing, not easily understood. This was a true partnership, not just friends with benefits. It must involve constant give and take. And it wasn't just about the sex in any case. It was about sharing a love to last a life-time. There was a big difference.

They lay together, with Stephanie spooning Alana from behind, and the sex had relaxed their bodies even more than their minds, so Alana fell asleep quickly. Steph lay awake for half an hour longer, pondering.

She didn't often ponder, but tonight she knew it was something she needed to do. It had been a tumultuous trip so far, but she guessed she had even more lessons to learn, and the weekend was not even half over.

The quest to find the girl on the plane, to rescue her from harm and restore her to those she loved. This had seemed impossible a week ago. But they had achieved it. She had felt almost like a super-hero and had achieved something really worthwhile.

That was on the outside. Now she had to achieve something equally impossible, to enter an even more impenetrable forest, get to grips with the puzzling fears she had about commitment, marriage and children deep inside her own mind.

When she had done that, she maybe could answer all Alana's questions and see if she could match up to her expectations, see if their partnership was simply a time-limited thing of beauty, a flower blooming in a spring meadow, or something which would last a lifetime.

The 'signs' she'd been given, Granny Byrne's revelations and advice, Marie's little lecture, Sophie's sadness at facing old-age with no partner, and no children, and finally Ally's sudden assertiveness in bed just now, all of these she recognised as valid challenges to the emotional walls she's built up since her Dad had walked out all those years ago.

Steph was no fool, she understood her own fears and foibles, but sorting them out was going to be a daunting task. Was she ready at last to be the lover Alana deserved? Was she ready to commit to something even deeper than their current coupledom?

Turning all these things over in her mind prevented her sleeping as peacefully as Alana, curled up in front of her. Steph gently released her arm and stretching, lengthened her body to reach her toes down to the end of the bed. She felt the edge of the mattress, the end of their domain, and was happy she was warm and cosy, as well as cocooned under the duvet with her beautiful girlfriend.

"I'm so lucky..." was her last conscious thought as she turned over and went to sleep on her stomach, like a little child.

Chapter 23

Quelle surprise!

It was Sunday morning in Brussels, and apart from the need to call Jenni to see how Leontine and Patience were recovering, they expected to have a day of leisure. Marie had made it clear that she hoped to have the day at home with her children, and Sophie was keen to give her visitors a tour round some of the tourist sights of the city. As neither woman had been before, both Stephanie and Alana were very happy with this prospect.

Over breakfast, not croissants this morning, but Sophie's home-made crêpes with strawberry preserves, accompanied by more of her excellent coffee, they learned something about the sights they might see. But then Steph's phone rang unexpectedly.

It was Marie-Krystina, sounding very energetic, despite it supposedly being her day off.

"I've been making some phone calls to save you the bother," she said. "Jenni reports that she had a good night in a reclining chair, and the girls slept through the night for a full ten hours. She thinks they are showing few signs of trauma and could be released from hospital later today."

"That's great news, but where can they stay? Sophie's flat is bursting with just us being here," said Steph.

Marie said "I have a friend with a bigger house who is willing to accommodate them and Sister Jenni as well, for as long as it takes to get them proper papers. We are lucky we will be allowed to take care of them, as the social services and migrant agencies won't open until Thursday of this week, on January 2nd. But I have given Sophie's name with mine as their temporary guardians, and we are well known to the authorities.

I'll drive to Antwerp later and fetch them all back to Brussels. That's the plan. I also have some warm clothes we can give them."

"But what about your children? Don't you need to stay home with them?"

Marie replied, "I've thought of that and I wondered if I could drop them off with you all before I go. They're good kids and they know their way round Brussels very well. You could maybe take them round the Christmas markets or to one of the big parks together. I shouldn't be more than a few hours."

"That will be fine," said Stephanie. "Ally especially has a pied-piper ability to charm children. I'm sure we'll be able to think of some fun things to do."

"They know Sophie as well. She's almost their honorary Granny."

"Great."

"Yes, but I have more, even more positive news. My friend in the police called last night to tell me that one of the traffickers they picked up in the dawn raid yesterday has continued to give them information in return for some deal over his charges.

"But this is the killer deal. He says he will tell them the identity of the man who murdered Carrie Montarini, and even more importantly, he said that the man is probably among the gang the Antwerp police picked up yesterday when we rescued Leontine. The informant is going to be interrogated again today, and the detectives are building up the case."

Steph said, "If that's the situation, then we really need to ask Isabel to come to Brussels. She has a huge dossier on Carrie's murder which she compiled after it happened. She just couldn't convince the police in Moldova to arrest the prime suspect in time, and so he disappeared back to the west over the border into Romania."

Marie nodded. "I agree it's time she knew all about this, and this is my main reason for calling you so early. You will have Bel's number, won't you? Can you see if you can get hold of her, and ask her to come to Brussels tomorrow? The police here are very keen to make progress on the trafficking charges, but if they have evidence that one of the detainees is also a suspect in a murder enquiry, then they can extend the time they have them in custody. This could be crucial in finally nailing the bastard, and getting justice for Isabel."

"Yes, I'll do it now, and I won't give up until I find her. She'll be fired up when she hears this."

Steph relayed the information in the phone call to Ally and Sophie and they both shared her hope that this might be a turning point for Isabel in her three year search for justice. Then Alana did a little calculation.

"It's Sunday December 29th today. Isabel and Bryony went on their honeymoon on the 18th. So they must surely be back home in London by now. Call them, Steph, and let's see if they can come tomorrow. You should meet Bryony, Steph. She's lovely."

So Steph picked up her freshly charged IPhone and called Isabel's private mobile number, known only to a very few trusted friends. Success! It was picked up after only three rings."

"Steph! How are you? Where are you?"

"I'm in Brussels, Bel. More to the point, where are you? Could you get over here by tomorrow? We have very exciting news for you."

"Bryony and I returned early from our honeymoon in Wales, because she was on duty at the hospital over Christmas. So we're here in Highbury, still snuggled up in bed, if you must know. But it's good to hear from you. What's the news you are so keen to share on a cold and wintry Sunday morning?"

Stephanie took a deep breath, and brought her boss up to speed with all the events of the Christmas holidays. It was quite a saga, from meeting the girl on the train, tracing the number she'd slipped across to her on a scrap of paper, hearing from Sister Jenni in Canada, collecting her from Heathrow then making a joint trip on Eurostar to Brussels, finding the girls and rescuing them along with the Police, and now having a very strong lead to Carrie's murderer! It was some adventure, and she couldn't believe it had all taken place in just ten days.

Isabel heard her out patiently, then just responded with a "Wow!" She then reverted to her normal, quick-thinking and imperious self. "No, we're not waiting till tomorrow. We will come to join you in Brussels today!"

Steph could hear Bel turn sideways and say, "Darling, get yourself out of bed and book us two seats on the next available Eurostar to Brussels. Oh and look up suitable hotels as well." And then Steph heard someone, presumably Bryony, laugh and say, "O.K, great Queen, normal service resumed." And sound of someone moving around and leaving the room.

Isabel came back on the line. "Now then, tell me more. Where are you staying in the city, and how are the other victims of the traffickers?"

Steph told Isabel all about Marie-Krystina, Jenni, Sophie and all about their adventures. She also said, "Ally is with me as well. She's been wonderful. We are having a day sight-seeing with Marie-Krystina's children today, but we can include both of you if you can get here in time."

"I'll call you back as soon as we know which train we can catch. We live only one stop north of St Pancras, as you know, so we should be able to be there by early afternoon. I'll bring all the paperwork I have on the murder, as well as what I have online. Oh and book us somewhere for dinner, where we can include everyone. It will be my treat. I want to show off my beautiful new wife to you all!"

Marie and her children arrived within the hour, and there were hugs and kisses exchanged all round. Sophie in particular opened her arms and let the children in for a big hug. The two girls and a boy all seemed to love her, almost as if she was their grandmother, so Steph was relieved. Sophie obviously did have some young people in her life.

"Their affection for her has come through baby-sitting for me so often," remarked Marie. "When I first split up from my husband, she was our guardian angel, and enabled me to carry on working. Much of our work involves being out late at night, looking for the girls at work on the streets, and Sophie often stayed over to put the children to bed."

"I think if Alana and I ever had children, we'd need excellent child-care help like that," said Steph, without thinking. But then she realized she was actually entertaining the idea that one day they might do it, they too might become parents. She had never even let the thought enter her head before.

"Well, I hope my children all behave well and don't put you off the idea for life! Now I must go. I will see you all back here at 5 pm?"

Ally spoke up now. "We managed to get hold of Isabel who has just texted to confirm she and her wife will be in Brussels by 3 pm. They've booked into one of those new hotels in the Euro quarter, but she wants to take us all out for dinner. Can you and the children come as well?"

Marie looked at her kids, bouncing on and off Sophie's sofa. "That's a very nice idea. It isn't a school day tomorrow, so I guess we can all stay up a little later than normal. Does 5pm still work for you in that case? What about Leontine and the other young African? We will have to include them, but will they want to come? If not, then I know Jenni will insist she stays with them."

"Bel asked us to book somewhere. Can you think of a quiet restaurant which is child-friendly and where the Africans won't feel too exposed?"

"I know the place! It is an African-owned restaurant down in Marolles, and I from what I remember, we can have the whole back room to ourselves. It will be quiet on the Sunday after Christmas. I'll see if they are open and give them the numbers."

Steph counted everyone up on her fingers and came to an answer. "Twelve".

"That's quite a party, but I wondered if we could also include my two colleagues." said Marie, "They are as committed to the welfare of trafficked girls as much as I am, and will be so happy to meet you all. We can pay our own way."

This seemed a good plan. Marie promised to ring the restaurant, then she disappeared back down the long stone stairs, and the women were left to amuse the three children. The oldest girl, called Agnes, took charge of the younger ones, and said to Alana in careful English.

"Hello. How do you do? My name is Agnes, and this is my sister Clotilde, and my brother Frederico. I am ten years old,

Clotilde has eight years and Freddie has six."

Alana beamed at her. "Thank you, Agnes, your English is very good, but it is better practice for us if you speak in French as you would normally. Then we can improve, and you can correct us if we say things wrong."

Agnes looked very relieved and also pleased to be thought so grown-up that she could teach these grown-ups. Her attempt at good English seemed to have already worn her out a little and she was obviously making a big effort to remember the lessons she had had in school.

Sophie then began to talk in French, volubly, and the children slipped off their coats, hats and gloves. Little Freddie had already slipped his hand into Ally's. She certainly did have the charm of the Irish about her when it came to small children.

It took them an hour or two before they left the apartment to begin their sight-seeing tour, as Sophie said there was no point being out in the cold before various galleries and museums were open. In the meantime they amused the children and themselves at the kitchen table by making some gingerbread people.

Alana solved their lack of a cookie template, but drawing her own on a piece of card, and then showing the children how to cut carefully round it with a blunt knife. From the dough which Sophie mixed up and Steph rolled out with Agnes's help, they were able to create twelve little people.

Clotilde and Freddie were given some currants and made the eyes and buttons up the cookies' fronts. Sophie also set them to greasing some old but good quality baking trays and they carefully transferred their little creations onto it. Then Sophie opened the oven door and Ally slid the trays inside.

"Ten minutes may be enough," said Ally. "We need to watch the oven to see that they don't burn."

The children admitted they had never cooked anything before, and obviously found the whole activity great fun. In the time it took to wash up the dishes and wipe down Sophie's kitchen tops, the smell of ginger and cinnamon had wafted round the kitchen, telling everyone the cookies were ready, and Sophie pulled out the sheet pan with something of a flourish. She transferred the gingerbreads onto a cooling rack.

Meanwhile Ally had stirred up a little pan of white icing with powdered sugar and a touch of boiling water. Then she snipped the end off a small plastic bag, filled it with the icing, and showed the children how to draw smiley mouths and eyebrows on each one. Steph held little Freddie back from the table, frightened he might burn his fingers, but he demanded to have a go, and in the end each child had a ginger person in his or her image, with letters on them, A, C and F. "We will leave them to show your Maman when she returns," said Sophie." Well done, everyone. You are all magnificent chefs!"

A Girl on the Plane

Chapter 24

So much to see.

Touring the city of Brussels on a wintry Sunday just after Christmas, might not have seemed too enticing a prospect for three small children and two British women, but they all had a crazy and totally enjoyable time. Sophie said, "We have to start with the Grand Place. It's the centre of everything, and then we can explore the Christmas markets. They are said to be the best in Europe."

They took two trams down to the huge square, surrounded by fascinating medieval buildings, and jumped off to find themselves in the middle of some street performers, acting and singing and creating some sort of pantomime. It was great fun to watch, and the children loved the clowning about, especially when one guy, perched five feet up on stilts, tottered over to them and gave them each a balloon.

Then they explored along the lines of the street markets, and wandered all through the central area. Sophie had an itinerary in her head, and kept them to it, taking them to the huge Kiekenmarkt which once had been a vast market arena, but was now an art gallery complex.

The next stop was the famous puppet theatre which the children especially loved. Agnes and Clotilde had been there before but Freddie never had, and he was fascinated by the many different types of puppets. From there they took the subway four miles north from the centre, to the iconic Atomium Museum with its great glass globes looking like atomic structures. There would be enough there to keep them all occupied for most of the afternoon.

"But first, let's stop at the hot-dog stall for lunch,"

suggested Stephanie, feeling her stomach rumbling, and seeing a street stall selling the universal snacks. A delicious smell of smoked sausage and mustard was floating towards them, and the children jumped up and down with excitement.

Sophie nodded, "Yes, let's do that." They bought hotdogs all round, and some boxes of juice, and sat down on one of the fixed tables and chairs to eat the lot. Everyone was cold and hungry for something warm, and even little Freddie finished his hot-dog in double quick time.

"Yumyumyum," he seemed to be saying, or maybe the equivalent in French. They spent five minutes more, finishing the scratch lunch, and then Alana gathered up the paper trays, napkins and juice boxes and disposed of them all in the waste bin.

"As we haven't even had time to visit the chocolate factory museum," she said, "This will have to do for now."

"I don't think the chocolate factory is open on Sundays," said Sophie. "Now let's go inside the museum. I think you will be impressed."

It was a wonderful modern museum, with so many interactive displays about science, how plastics were made, for example, and all sorts of fascinating activities that the children could have spent a week there.

"We will come again in the spring," promised Sophie to them. "But now we should make our way back to the city centre. When do you expect your friends?" she asked Stephanie.

Steph gulped and realized she'd turned off her phone, forgetting Bel would be calling. When she re-opened it, yes, there was a text message flashing.

"Arriving into Brussels South Station at 4.45pm. Meet you there?"

It was already nearly 4.00pm, and the museum was about to close.

"Come on everyone, we have to meet our friends! Let's go!"

They took the Line 1 subway train back into Brussels centre, and then transferred to the connecting line to Brussels Midi, which took a few minutes more. Steph had quickly written a reply to Isabel say they were on their way, and to wait for them on the platform. But in the end they ran up from the Metro at the precise moment the long Eurostar express drew into the station and pulled to a smooth halt.

"I can't believe it was only two days ago that we came over by the same means," said Alana. "So much has happened since!"

The doors in the train were all released simultaneously and passengers started to step out onto the platform and make their way towards the exit gates.

Sophie said, "I'm excited to meet your boss. She is quite famous, you know, an eco-warrior celebrity. Marie-Krystina has also told me so much about her."

The three women and three children formed quite a little welcoming party, but Steph felt a frisson of nerves which surprised her. She had known Bel Bridgford for seven years or more now, and counted her a close friend as well as an inspiring boss, but she knew she always would have a secret crush on her, more hero worship than anything else.

And they hadn't met in person since Isabel had started her sabbatical the previous January. They'd skyped for sure, but Isabel was always more powerful in person, and the last time she had zoomed her, she had still looked pitifully frail and quite tiny, she'd lost so much weight.

"There they are!" said Alana, looking down the platform. Steph gasped. Isabel looked a different woman from the frail convalescent from their last online meeting. As they approached, they exchanged waves and Steph could see just how brilliantly Isabel had healed after her horrible road accident. There had been rumours she'd never walk again, but here she was, looking undeniably fighting fit, and gorgeous.

Isabel now walked tall and free, without even a limp, her dark wavy hair, flicked back behind her ears, shone with health and her clear Irish blue eyes were as intense a violet colour as they'd ever been. She'd also put on a few pounds since before the accident, which suited her tremendously. With her fashionable long wool coat, black trousers and Cuban heeled boots, she looked a million dollars.

Just behind her walked a very beautiful and equally fit

young woman, taller, with a short honey-coloured crop of hair and an equally confident and cheerful style. So this was Bryony, Bel's new medical student wife. She was pulling a couple of small cases, so was obviously still assisting Isabel, but she didn't seem to mind. The pair kept exchanging warm smiles, and it was obvious to even the most casual observer that they were crazy about each other.

Isabel reached out and hugged and kissed both Steph and Alana, introduced Bryony to them, and was then introduced to Sophie, who declared herself a great fan, and said she felt quite shy in the company of the famous Isabel Bridgford.

"Au contraire," said Isabel, "It is I who am honoured. I know all about your work on the European Refugee Council. I am so happy to meet you, Sophie. Now, who are these poppets?"

"These are Marie-Krystina's children," said Alana. "May I introduce to you, Agnes, Clotilde and Frederick?"

The children shook hands like little professionals and especially pumped the hand of Bryony whom Isabel had drawn into the circle.

"You are a very beautiful lady!" pronounced Agnes, gazing up at Bryony, clearly quite smitten.

"She certainly is," agreed Isabel. "What a perceptive child you are. The last time I saw you, you were a baby. I am so looking forward to meeting your mother again."

Steph said, "We thought we would accompany you now to your hotel, and then we can all return to meet Marie Krystina, Sister Jenni, Leontine and Patience at Sophie's flat. They will be there by six, and then we can eat together. Marie has booked us into a restaurant I think you will like. It is run by Ghanaians so it has a great West African menus and ambience."

"Sounds great," said Bel. "Over the summer, Bryony and I moved towards Veganism, but I am sure there will be lots of food we will enjoy."

"Well, you certainly both look well on the new regime," said Stephanie. "Now then, remind me the name of the hotel you have booked into."

And they all moved towards the tram stops together.

***

When they returned to Sophie's place, the children were showing signs of obvious fatigue and happily nestled onto the sofa to watch a children's television channel. Then the street doorbell rang, to usher in the party returning from Antwerp. Marie Krystina came inside first, encouraging two very shy and very nervous looking West African girls, with Sister Jenni bringing up the rear.

The friendly domesticity of the apartment, and the sight of five women and three children obviously astonished Leontine and Patience. They were further overwhelmed by the way all the women approached them and hugged them in welcome. It was so alien to their culture, and so different from the institutional care in hospital they'd had over the last day or so. But they bore it well, and just naturally gravitated back to the edges of the room.

Jenni however urged them forward, and Alana showed them the gingerbread people the children and she and Sophie had produced and said, "Come, have one each. We cooked them this morning to celebrate you coming. You will like them."

Patience, who looked as though she hadn't enjoyed a moment's kindness or even a place to sit down in many months, picked one of the cookie characters up and turned to Jenni for permission to eat it.

"Of course. It's for you. They made them to celebrate you both leaving the hospital." She repeated it in Lingala, and both girls shyly began to nibble the cookies.

Steph's heart went out to them. She could see the shadow of what they had endured in their eyes, which they tended to keep downcast towards the floor. It was almost like the released political prisoners she had worked with in other countries, and she knew they would need intensive counselling and therapy if they were to recover fully from their ordeal.

Jenni then turned to Isabel and Bryony and was urged to tell her own story again. Isabel opened her arms and embraced her warmly, kissing her on both cheeks, and saying, "Oh, Jenni, Jenni! It's been too long. You will have heard about Carrie?"

"Yes, of course, and I hope you received my condolence letter. I have been too long in the Congo I'm afraid, so this is a wonderful bonus, to meet up with you again and also meet Bryony."

"Isabel's told me so much about you," said Bryony, smiling. "I'm only just coming to terms with how many friends she has all over the world, but I gather you and she worked together on a campaign to try to stop FGM ten years or so ago."

Jenni's eyes crinkled at the edges.

"One of many campaigns where I just floated behind her in her jet-stream. Your wife is phenomenal, but I'm sure you don't need me to tell you."

Bryony put her arms round Isabel's waist and pulled her close for a kiss. "No, perhaps, but I never tire of hearing it from other people. Having her as my wife is still unbelievable. I know I am the luckiest woman in the world."

Isabel, for all her self-assurance and style, did go a definite shade of pink at these words, and returned the kiss with interest. She looked so much like a woman in love, that Stephanie almost felt embarrassed for her.

But then she remembered how she and Alana had acted in their first months of coupledom. She had been especially tactile and couldn't keep her hands off her beautiful ice-queen. They had often been teased and told to 'get a room!'

But now she turned her head and saw Ally gazing at her with an uncannily similar focus to Isabel's on Bryony. There was real, deep love in those cool grey eyes, and she swallowed nervously. Was she good enough for Ally? Did she deserve her? These were questions which troubled her, as she honestly doubted she could answer them in the affirmative.

Then Ally's gaze turned away from her to the children on the sofa, and an unforced smile came over her face. She sat down beside them and asked them in French to tell her what they were watching, and was it a favorite of theirs? They began to chat happily to her. No doubt about it, Ally was a natural with children.

***

The African restaurant was perfect for their needs, and gave them a warm and congenial location for their evening together. Marie-Krystina's younger colleagues, Josephine and Claudette, joined them there, and they all sat round a large table.

The owners were delighted to have such a big party to cater for, and produced plate after plate of delicious chicken, fish, and vegetables dishes. Steph forgot her declaration to Ally that she never wanted to eat rice again and tucked into the Jollof rice dish with gusto. So did the two rescued girls, reassured at last by the sight and smell of food with which they were familiar.

Isabel sat between Stephanie and Ally, as she said she wanted to talk to them especially.

"I owe so much to both of you. Steph, you've achieved a wonderful job with our West African projects, and I'm well aware of all you've given, Ally, to secretly keep our show on the road financially. I thought I might give you the nickname "Anon" after seeing the regular large monthly donations which have come from you all year. After the climate change campaign, I'll be back full-time from January, and I have certain plans for Righteous Anger I want to share with you."

Steph in turn kept her voice low, to avoid Jenni at the other end of the table hearing too much, but said, "Bel, could we consider offering a position to Jenni when she's settled Leontine back at school in the DCR? She would be such a brilliant colleague to keep, and it would mean a lot less pressure for me not to have to cope with all the French speaking countries, and negotiating the funding partnerships there. She's not supposed to work in tropical countries any more, but I know she'd be wonderful as a desk officer in London with us."

Isabel looked down the table at the stern but kind features of a woman Steph knew she had admired for many years. "I think in principle it's a very good idea, if we can fit it into our budget. Let's see what she thinks, when we return to London. How long are you two aiming to stay in Brussels?"

Alana felt her cheeks go a little pink as a warm flush of panic rose up from her chest. "I have to be back at work from Thursday 2nd."

She didn't mention the make or break interview on Friday

January 3rd, and the thought of it filled her with a sudden huge melancholy.

If only she could trust Steph to be the partner she craved, then the big job interview wouldn't even be needed, but she just couldn't trust her heart to believe that. But she should tell her about it, to be only fair.

Chapter 25

Justice for Carrie.

The evening had ended early in order for the children to be taken home to bed, but it had undoubtedly been a great success. The camaraderie and friendship round the table between so many women of such different backgrounds and experiences had been almost tangible.

Little Freddie hadn't really noticed that he was the only male amongst so many females. Being the youngest was the one thing he had commented on, as he whispered to his mother, about which food he'd be allowed to eat. And he and her other children seemed to have swopped allegiance from Alana and Sophie to Bryony, who for some reason seemed to emit a magnetic attraction for them..

Later that night, as they sat in bed together in Sophie's flat, Steph mentioned this to Alana, adding, "The girl's so quiet, so measured and sensible, but she's effected a minor miracle where Bel is concerned. In all the years I've known her, even before Carrie died, I've never known her so happy, so lit up. I think she's really got through her bereavement at last, that Isabel's truly healed."

Alana agreed. "Yes, I don't think she'd have married Bryony if she didn't feel ready for it. There's such empathy between them, and it's obvious that Bryony thinks the sun shines out of Isabel. It's very sweet how caring she is of her, how she's watching all the time in case she might fall or looks in any way in pain."

"Yes, a smash up like that, even when the bones are healed, will be bound to cause residual aches and pains. I broke my ankle when I was twelve playing tennis, and it still twinges."

***

Twinges or not, when they met up with the other couple at *Sœurs de la férocité* offices early the following morning, Isabel was obviously in power mode. She had with her a large file full of the evidence and information she'd personally gathered about Carrie's murder, and as she explained to the others, she'd found something else when Bryony and she had gone through all Carrie's possessions in their flat.

"We found this. It wasn't her main mobile phone, retrieved when they found her body, but this is an older one, a spare maybe, but one we found at the bottom of a drawer. I charged it up, and low and behold, there is a whole library of photos from the enquiries she'd been making about trafficked girls brought over through Albania and Romania. There are half a dozen pictures of one man there, and I'm sure he was the one she had targeted as the prime suspect for the gang leader."

Isabel passed the pictures around, and Marie took in a sharp breath.

"This guy, he has crossed our radar twice before, and yes, he was one of the ones picked up from the Four Winds Hotel. We need to get down to the police with this straight away. I will call my friend on the vice squad and tell him."

She moved into the next room, where it was quieter and made the call. Steph and Ally looked at Bel and Bryony, and at the young staffers who had just arrived. Sophie had left to work at her Refugee and Migration agency, but they wondered where the others in their company were.

"Do we know where Sister Jenni and the girls are this morning?"

Josephine answered, "They are also going to the police headquarters to make more official witness statements. I think the girls will be needed when the case goes to court, so this may mean that Sister Jenni has to stay in Belgium with them for several months. She told me this last night."

"I am worried she won't have enough funds," said Alana.

"No, it's OK," she told me her Order has millions of dollars in the bank and that they will support her to stay over here and care for the girls. They were left a very large property portfolio in Canada, and the interest alone will fund anything she needs. She says most of the nuns are very elderly now, and live very quietly. She is the only activist left!" Josephine had been seated next to Jenni at the dinner, and had obviously enjoyed getting to know more about her, and what made her able to travel and come to Europe.

Marie then emerged from her office and announced, "The police are very keen to see us all, especially Isabel. Let's go!"

Five of them went to the police headquarters dealing with the kidnapping and trafficking arrests, and were pleased to see Jenni and her young charges in one of the waiting rooms. The girls smiled when they saw them, and seemed much less traumatized and nervous than they had before. While they all waited to be seen by different officers, Jenni brought the others up to date with some news.

"I have been on to the people at Social Services, and they are looking out for some foster parents for both the girls, while they are based here. I told them we need a rock-solidly reliable Congolese or Nigerian family, resident in Brussels, where they can be with other Africans and enjoy the company of younger people, not just a weathered old Canadian white woman. We are going round there later to see what they have managed to deliver. Of course I am not letting either of them out of my sight until I know they will be safe and well-looked after. If no-one suitable is found, then I will stay here with them myself."

"It's a great idea. If it works out, then you can come to join us in London later," said Isabel. "Steph has already suggested you join us at Righteous Anger, and if your religious order could support you in post, as Josephine seemed to think they might, then it would be even better!"

"Sounds good to me. Let's discuss it further, when all this trouble is behind us," answered Jenni, pushing her hands through her thick, wavy mop of hair, and they left it like that, but on a very positive note.

Then two police officers appeared at the same time, one to escort Jenni and the girls through to another interview room, and the other, a bright looking woman out of uniform, came forward to shake Isabel's hand as she greeted the whole bunch of them.

"Please, come with me. I'm the senior detective. I have been following your case on Interpol and I think we have a real breakthrough here."

Isabel, Bryony and Marie stood up to go with her, and Alana and Stephanie realized they weren't really needed in any way.

"Why don't we go off to take breakfast somewhere?" asked Steph. "Call us when you're through and we'll return then."

It seemed a good plan, and she and Alana left their friends and headed off to the nearest open café where a chef was creating the famously good Belgian waffles.

They sat down at a table in the window, ordered two cafés au lait and the extra-large waffle deal, complete with chocolate sauce and whipped cream. Alana looked across at Steph, gorgeous as ever, with her everlasting golden tan, her tawny mop of hair and her "come hither" eyes. They had been reunited now for at least ten days, and it had been really good in terms of the fantastic sex they'd enjoyed.

But the big conundrum between them still hadn't really been addressed. Maybe now, in a semi-public setting, over the best coffee and a delicious breakfast, was as good a time as any to spill the beans about her job offer in New York.

Steph had nipped out to use the toilet, and when she returned, Alana screwed up every bit of courage she had inside her and said.

"Steph, there's something I haven't told you. The time hasn't been right somehow."

"What?"

She could tell Steph's antennae were already flashing wildly.

"Well, a few weeks ago, some people from an international recruitment agency got in touch with me at work, and made me a proposal, one I'm sure I won't accept, but I felt I should talk it over with you."

Stephanie looked shocked, but then the waiter came to their table with two wide bowls of white coffee in the French style, and gave them the cutlery and napkins ready for their waffles.

When he'd retreated, Steph said, "So, what is it?

Headhunted by another accountancy giant? Was this why you don't want to be the one who carries our child?"

Alana was a little surprised she had even mentioned the baby. Steph hadn't thrown the idea completely away then. This would make what she had to say, even more painful.

"Not an accountancy firm, no. But something more in your field. You've heard about *Financial International Response for Emergencies?*"

"You mean *FIRE.* Of course, it's a global giant, as big as *Oxfam* or *Save the Children.* It has offices all over the world."

"Well, they have an opening for a CFO. They want to discuss it with me, on Thursday of this week, by Skype."

"Not in person, not at their London office?"

"No, well you see, if I took the post, (and it is a very big If,) I'd have to be based at their head office. . ."

"And that's where . . ."

Alana could see Steph already knew the answer to that question.

"New York."

For a few seconds they pretended this wasn't the bombshell it was. Both of them smiled at the returning waiter as he deposited two steaming and delicious looking piles of waffles in front of them, and squirted cream in a flourish over the plates.

Steph was clearly struggling to analyze what she'd just been told.

"If, you say 'If'. Haven't you already decided?"

"No, not at all. It depends what you think, what you want."

"But you are taking it seriously? It's been on the cards for you?"

"Yes, I'd be lying if I said otherwise. Steph, it's not what I want, but if you don't want honestly to build a family with me, to commit to us being together for life, then this might be the least painful way for us both to admit it. I love and need you so much, and I told you the truth that I can't carry on as before, with you never being here. If you can't or won't change, then maybe I should be the one to leave. And this job would be so huge, so challenging it might keep me from going mad with grief. Anyway, I might not even be offered the position, once they see how unimpressive I am at the interview."

Steph snorted with derision at that silly idea. "Of course they will offer you the job. You are the best in London at what you do, and drop-dead gorgeous as well. One look at you, and they'll be couriering over a contract for you to sign within the hour."

"So…what do you think I should do?"

Alana sounded and felt completely vulnerable. There was a painful silence, while they both ate a few mouthfuls of their waffles.

Finally, Steph said quietly, looking down at her plate, "I don't know what you should do. I need time to think about this, honey. You have thrown such a curved ball at me. No I'm not mad at you," as she caught Alana's anxious eye, "I have understood how deeply you've been feeling, even though I've snapped at you when you've tried to talk about it. It's not you…"

"Please don't say, 'It's not you, it's me.' You know where those conversations go."

Steph stopped her and said, "I know, but I think that it is true in our case. I've had so many personal issues. I can't blame you for wanting to scream at me at times. But this Christmas, I think we've been closer than we've been for more than a year. We are being honest about our differences and what our needs are. That's good. And one thing has been made blindingly obvious to me."

"What?"

"I really, really love you, Ally."

"I love you too, Steph."

Alana could say it honestly, and she believed Steph was honest too. But why was there still such a void between them. Why wasn't Steph saying more? Why wasn't she offering what she must know Alana needed to hear? Why wasn't she proposing, goddamnit?"

"Just give me some time to think it through," was the best Ally could get out of Steph. They finished their waffles, drank their coffees, paid the bill, and began to prepare to wander back to the police station together.

Steph grabbed Alana's gloved hand and held it as they

walked back up the street. But a deep sadness seemed to fall over them both. They loved each other, but maybe that wasn't enough to go forward together anymore. Alana mentally began to prepare a list of questions to ask at her interview. Moving to New York and leaving Stephanie was truly the last thing in the world she wanted to do right now, but what if it was her only option?

Chapter 26

A shoulder to cry on.

Isabel and Bryony emerged from the Police Headquarters interview suite two hours later to find Steph sitting alone reading in the waiting room.

"Where's Alana?" asked Bryony, posing the obvious question.

"She has gone back into the city centre, to the fashion quarter, to look at the spring collections. Ally always likes fashion much more than I do. She says she'll meet us tonight."

Steph didn't tell them the whole story, how their joint mood had descended into definite misery after waiting together in silence for thirty minutes, and how Ally had taken the initiative to break their impasse and declared she was taking a tram to have the rest of the day to herself. She hadn't exactly sprinted to get away from Steph, but it had felt like that. Steph saw it as a foretaste of how life would be when they returned to London.

Despite all their beautiful sex, despite everything Ally had said, Steph could feel in her bones she was going to get dumped, that Ally would ditch her before she did the same to her. She felt as small and as lost as she ever had, worse even, if it was possible, than when her father had walked out. But she felt paralysed, unable to do what she so wanted to do to make everything better.

"How did you two get on?" she asked, "And where's Marie?"

Isabel said, "Marie has returned to Antwerp with the chief investigating officer. It seems my additional evidence, along with the images on the phone, might just have turned the case around. They think they have enough evidence to prosecute the man we know killed Carrie, and they've gone to set up another round of interrogations for him. At last, I can get closure and justice for my darling girl."

"Isabel, I'm so happy for you! It might be an end to the nightmare at last."

"Fingers crossed, anyway. We'll know finally in a month or so, but for now, my work here is done. I've handed them all my files, and they did seem genuinely grateful."

Bryony nodded and said, "Isn't it wonderful? But I'm afraid I have to return to our hotel now. I have a long assignment to submit in a couple of weeks and this is my only free time to study. Will you two be OK if I leave you for the rest of the day?"

Isabel nodded, "Of course, darling. Steph and I will be fine. We have so much to catch up on.

So Bryony disappeared in the direction of the Metro, and Isabel took Steph's arm and said, "Come, walk with me. I think we need to talk."

Steph's eyebrows raised. Was she that obvious? She felt so emotional that even more than simply talking, she wanted to burst into tears. Isabel linked their arms together and pulled her outside into the chilly, but dry day.

Then Isabel squeezed her arm and said, "Come and keep my company for a walk round that park opposite, and tell me what's up. You look like you've lost a pound and picked up a shilling, as my old granny used to say."

The park was one of Brussels' many green spaces, and they walked together through the gates. Steph wondered how much she should say to her boss, or what she should say at all. Her mind was in such turmoil. But in the end, Isabel's calm but firm presence gave her some confidence and she began to talk honestly and quietly about everything Ally had said to her since she'd returned from the Congo.

"She says she's lonely and forlorn with me away so much, that things can't continue as they are. She wants me to change my job somehow so I'm home more. And then she said two things which have floored me. She tells me that for months now she's been yearning for us to have a child together, and she wants me to be the one who gets pregnant and carries it! Can you imagine me as a mum? I'd be completely useless.

"And now, finally, this morning, she's just let me know she's been approached about a job as Head of Finance for *International Response*, in New York! If I don't agree to her terms, I think she'll take the job, and move away to America. I'll so frightened I'll lose her, Isabel, and I don't know what to do!"

Isabel reached across with her other hand, the one which wasn't linked through Steph's arm, and gently rubbed her cold fingers. It was such a gentle touch, an almost sisterly or motherly mark of affection, that it made Steph feel the prickle of tears behind her eyes, and had to sniff to stop her voice breaking.

Isabel's tone was soft, but her words were hard enough to go to the heart of the problem.

"What are you exactly telling me, Steph, that you don't want to make a long-term commitment to Alana, or that you feel you can't, for some reason?"

"I do want to. God, I want to so much. I told her I hoped we'd be together for thirty years."

"So in that case, let's perhaps look at why you feel you can't..."

They walked slowly through the park, which even in winter was beautiful. It was quiet and almost empty, with just a few dog walkers in the distance.

"Well, I have done my own processing about this over the last week or so. It doesn't take a genius to know the reason I'm totally screwed up about childbirth, is because I saw my mother have a traumatic miscarriage when I was only five years old, and I'm scared of being left because of my Dad leaving the family when I was thirteen. It's taken me twenty years to get over that!

"But now I'm thirty-three, and I'm thinking, maybe I can't commit because I'm frightened that I'm more like my Dad than I have ever admitted. What if I marry Alana and then let her down, leave her eventually, abandon her and our child or children? That's my real nightmare. And I don't know what to do, if I can't trust myself."

There. She had actually said it out loud, her worst fear, not that Ally would leave her, but that she would be the one to fail, to be selfish and inadequate, and absent.

Isabel beckoned to a vacant seat a little way ahead. "I could do with a sit-down if you don't mind. My leg throbs sometimes after walking for a while."

They moved to the seat, but Isabel still held Stephanie close to her.

"You know, I've always thought Alana has excellent taste, in everything."

"Hmm?"

"And she is such a sensible and level-headed woman…"

"Yes…"

"And brilliant at decision making…"

"Absolutely…"

"And she chose you. So if you doubt your own character and decision-making ability, Steph, why not rely on hers?"

Isabel gave Stephanie a wry little smile.

"She trusts you, and the future you two could build together, but she wants you to trust in it as well. I have to say though, in any case, I don't recognise the person you've just described to me at all.

"I don't believe you would ever desert Alana, that you wouldn't be a wonderful parent. She's told you what she needs, and that you are the person to give it to her, so believe her, if you can't believe in yourself."

"You think so? I mean, you think I should have more faith in myself?"

"Completely. I can see how much you've matured, how much more self-aware you are now than when I went off on Sabbatical a year ago. Trust in yourself, Steph, and see what a lovely person you are.

"Look, follow my example! I was so judgmental of myself, so pessimistic that I even deserved to be loved, that I actually pushed Bryony away at the end of August, after we had had a beautiful summer together, and I knew she was in love with me. I mistrusted my motives so much, that I nearly jeopardized our whole future together. Thank God she stayed true and was more sensible than I was. After three weeks I crawled back to her, and begged forgiveness."

"And what did she say?"

"She proposed to me immediately. I am still on cloud nine four months later."

"Wow."

"Yes. So don't listen to those voices in your head, Stephanie. Follow your heart, and follow Alana. I can see how much you love each other. And as for babies, well, take first things first. Say out loud the commitment you already feel in your heart, and then, when and if you decide together to have a child, you will have a firm foundation for having a family. If you are still frightened then of the physical process, there are many different options, aren't there? There are children all over the world crying out for loving parents."

This last idea was one that Stephanie hadn't had before, and it put a whole new perspective on things. Maybe they could adopt! It lifted that constriction of panic from her chest. She walked arm in arm with Isabel again, and they made their way to the subway station, parting company when they needed to take different trains.

"So, are you going home tonight?" she asked her boss, at the barrier gates.

"No, but first thing tomorrow. I'm done here, and Bryony needs to go back to the hospital. She's on duty again over the New Year."

"Will you both come round to our flat soon for a meal? I promised Ally I'd invite you sometime later in January."

"Of course. We'd love to. In the meantime, I'll see you at the office later in the week."

They kissed, and parted, and Steph watched as Isabel's pretty face and elegant figure disappeared into the crowds. Only as she walked towards her own train, did she realize she had spoken as though she and Ally would still be together in the New Year. In her heart, she had automatically assumed it, and where her heart had led, now her mind followed. She had to stop Alana leaving, whatever the cost and whatever the consequences!

Well, if that was to be the case, then she knew it was down to her. She had to do something to make it happen. Rather than boarding the train, she turned on her heel and ran back up the steps to the surface, to do some shopping of her own.

Chapter 27

Deep Blue Hyacinths.

It was nearly six when she rang the doorbell for Sophie's block of flats, and heard Alana's light voice through the intercom. The door clicked open and she began to climb the stairs. Sophie had entrusted her spare door-key to Alana, wisely, as Steph knew her tendency to lose keys the moment they were entrusted to her.

So at least Ally had come home, not gone off to drink herself silly in some anonymous bar. Dear, sensible, stoical Ally, good at managing things, at managing loneliness. Steph was determined she wouldn't have to manage their relationship on her own anymore. When she reached the top floor, she banged on the apartment door with her elbow, because her hands were full.

Alana opened the door. She looked tense and pale, but managed a smile. Steph walked in; her arms were full of parcels and she was also balancing a large pot of deep blue hyacinths.

"Hello. Look, I bought these for Sophie, as a good-bye present. Don't they smell divine?"

She put them carefully in the centre of the dining table, and then went through into their guest bedroom, to drop off her other purchases.

"Wow. You have been shopping as well!" she said.

On the bed and hanging from the wardrobe were several new, designer-sharp outfits. Ally, who normally never spent serious money on clothes other than her immaculate and well-made business suits, had certainly splurged. There were some lovely dresses, and Steph immediately wished she could undress and dress her girl-friend up in them, one by one.

"Displacement activity," muttered Alana, looking at her with a bleak sadness. Steph couldn't bear it, not for a moment longer. She flung off her jacket, went forward, and pulled Ally into her arms. Alana resisted, protested even, and tried to push Steph away, but Steph refused to release her.

"Listen, listen to me. I've been thinking, hard. I know I've been an idiot, about this whole thing, about you, about us, about the future. But I know now, what the right way forward is."

Alana looked at her, her grey eyes giving nothing away, but her hands stopped pushing against Steph's chest. She opened her eyes wide, waiting for an answer.

Steph said, "I think you should go to your interview on Thursday, and if they offer you the job, I think you should take it."

Alana gave a little cry, almost like a kitten mewing. It was heart-breaking.

"No, I haven't finished!" said Steph, "Listen. It will be great! You should accept the New York job, and I'll….Ally, I want you to take me with you! And for me to get into the States, you'll need to make an honest woman of me, so I can travel with you as your spouse. I want us to get married, Ally. I want that, whether or not you take the job. Deep down, I know I've always wanted it. I've just been so stupid, so locked in the past."

Alana's expression was changing from misery to uncomprehending joy in front of her eyes. Steph wished she could film it, it was so miraculous.

"But...? Your work, your vocation at Righteous Anger? You said..."

"I know and I was an idiot. I haven't taken a vow of lifelong commitment to one organisation, like Sister Jenni. Righteous Anger will be fine without me. Did you know more graduates want to work in international development than in any other sector right now? Isabel could fill my post in a week. And America is surely packed full of non-governmental development agencies and campaigning groups. I'm sure I'll pick something up to keep me busy, while you're running the world. The main thing is that we can be together, on a new adventure."

"But you still don't want a baby...?"

"Who says I don't? A girl can change her mind, can't she? Look at my parcels. I went into one of those amazing boutiques for babies they have over here, and couldn't resist some of those tiny little outfits. I wanted to show you, how much you can spend on a new-born baby if you're ridiculously reckless. They cost a fortune, so we shouldn't waste them! We might either have to try to adopt, or I just might have to get over myself and do as you say, and explore the whole business of finding a donor and getting myself pregnant."

She released Alana, who sat down on the bed with a thump, as though her legs wouldn't support her any longer. Then she pulled open her bags and produced some tiny, exquisite things for babies, 0 to 3 months. She'd paid at least 150 Euros on what might be called a whole layette. It was ridiculous, extravagant and adorable.

Alana fingered the white silk dresses and little socks, almost as if she was in a trance. She was mesmerised into silence. Then she said, "This is the silliest thing I've ever known you do. You're insane."

Steph pressed on. "Quite probably, but I feel more grounded than I have in years. I've stopped running. From my past, from my mother and father's unhappiness, and from you. I know what I want, Ally. I want you. And I want our future together."

Stephanie knelt on the carpet in front of Alana and took her hands.

"But as I said, I want to do things right. I'm asking you to marry me, darling, just as I should have done when I chased after you three years ago. Will you have me, messy, careless, and forgetful as I am, for better, for worse, and all that jazz? Please say yes, please do . . ."

"Yes." Alana almost croaked the words out. "Yes, of course I will." Then she promptly burst into tears. Steph looked up into Ally's eyes, and shook her head.

"Don't cry, darling, don't cry. I know I've been a total pain in the arse, but I promise I'll improve. Look, instead of going straight back to London tomorrow, why don't we take a train up to Antwerp?"

"Antwerp, why?" Alana's face was still flushed and wet from crying, but she was no longer sobbing her heart out.

"Because it's the diamond capital of the world, and I am going to buy you the best, the biggest ring we can find there."

"Don't be silly," sniffed Ally. "I don't need fancy rings. I only want you. So please come back up here and kiss me."

So Stephanie reached up and did as she was told.

After a few moments, she said, "Now, I want to see you in each of these new outfits. I hope and assume you bought them to wear on dates with me! Let's have a little fashion show, and I'll tell you which one I like the best.

When Sophie came home from work half an hour later, the guest room door was still shut, and she could hear muffled laughter and an occasional scream of protest coming from inside.

She saw the new pot of blue hyacinths on the table, and inhaled their heady scent, and then went to turn on the oven for supper. It was lovely having the English girls to stay and she'd feel lonely after they left. Maybe she should get herself a kitten, just for company. She'd always liked cats. That was it, she should certainly get herself a kitten!

Epilogue

Conversations.

Steph picked up the phone and dialled very hesitantly. This was a call she'd been needing to make for days.

"Hi, Mum, now don't get excited. But how would you like to come to a wedding?"

"A wedding? Whose wedding?"

"Whose wedding? Well, ours of course. Ally's and mine!"

"So, you're finally going to do it?"

"Yes, we've set the date, a week or two before she begins her new job in New York, Saturday March 21st. You know she's had to give her current firm three months' notice, and she starts at *FIRE* on April 6st, so we are flying straight out after the wedding, and using our honeymoon to find an apartment to rent somewhere close to downtown New York."

"Wow. I never thought you would seriously get married!"

"What do you mean, you didn't think I was serious? Mum, I've never been more serious in my life. So make sure the date is in your diary, and we hope you will come down to London to stay with us for a few days before. You must visit us in New York as soon as we're settled, as well."

"Of course I'll come...but do you mind if I bring someone with me?"

"Can you 'bring someone with you' to the wedding? Yes, of course you can. I hope the whole family will come as well."

"This person isn't exactly family."

"Oh, you mean you want to 'bring someone new...a friend'? Who is she?"

"This person isn't a she, darling."

"Oh, so it's a 'he', that's nice. Who is he?"

"He's a tree-surgeon."

"A surgeon, did you say?"

"No...I said he is a *tree*-surgeon."

"Oh...a *tree*-surgeon. Is he the guy who came just after Christmas to cut down your trees? When you said surgeon, I just thought you meant..."

""Don't be so snobby, Stephanie. It's an honest living."

"Mum, I'm not being snobby at all. Of course I approve. I'm really happy for you. You sound so cheerful! Er...how old is this new boyfriend by the way?"

"He's forty-four."

"Forty- four!"

"Why do you sound so shocked? Just because there's snow on the roof doesn't mean there isn't a fire still burning in the hearth!"

"No, I'm *not* shocked Mum, *honestly*! Oh, and by the way that is *way* too much information!"

"Joanne and Craig don't approve. They think I'm too old to date a younger man."

"Well, don't listen to Joanne and Craig then, and don't let them bully you! I'm totally delighted for you. Ally will be too. Go for it, girl!"

"Thank you, Steph. That means a lot to me. I love you!"

"Yes, I love you too! 'Bye!"

As Steph put down the phone Alana came through the door, carrying a bag full of groceries from the supermarket she'd passed on the way home from the tube station. She plopped the whole load down on the kitchen table.

Steph, who had arrived home thirty minutes earlier, already had their flat tidied, candles lit and the table laid up for four people.

"Did you manage to get all the ingredients you needed, Ally?"

"Yes, lentil moussaka bake coming up, followed by apple crumble and coconut cream. I just have to take my coat off, and then we can get the show on the road. It will be so good to have Bel and Bryony here for dinner this evening. We can celebrate the trial date being set for Carrie's shooter, and tell them all about our plans for New York."

Steph took Ally's coat and hung it up in the hall cupboard.

"Wow, who are you and what have you done with my fiancée?"

"I keep telling you. Reformed character. I also rang my mum like you told me to, to tell her we've settled on the date for the wedding, and guess what?"

"Yes?"

"She hasn't only gone and got herself atoy-boy! And she asked if she could bring him as her plus-one to the wedding!"

"What?"

"Yes, he's the guy who came to work on her trees, and she says he's a hunk of forty-four!"

"Seriously?"

"Yes, and she sounds really happy. I can't believe it!"

"Good for Trudy. I must call her, and find out all the low-down on this guy, and how their romance started."

"Yeah, I bet she'll be less cagey talking to you about it than with me. You always have been able to communicate with her better."

"Now, don't start that up again! You can chat much more easily to my ferocious Granny Byrne than I can. She's another person who won't want to miss our wedding!"

"If everyone on our list comes, it will be a very eclectic affair!"

"Yes, it certainly will. Now, please come and help me unpack these groceries, and pull a bottle of the red wine out of the rack to warm up, there's a dear."

Their two guests arrived on time, laughing and shuffling their boots against the cold, and the dinner party progressed with lots of laughs, multiple expressions of appreciation for the food and drink, and a general feeling of good humour.

As they all tucked into the dessert Isabel said, waving her spoon over the pudding, "I had a long email from Jenni today. She says the legal business in Belgium is now settled, and the children have official leave to remain there at least until after the trial date, and all the final checks are done. They have both fitted happily into their foster homes, and are both even going to school, so she's free now, until she returns for the trial, whenever that is set for."

"So can you arrange for her to come to work with us?" asked Steph.

"Yes, I'm onto it," Bel replied. "I'll apply for a work permit for her. She can take over your desk, on an informal pro-bono basis for now, as her Canadian convent will cover her salary, so it will save us a substantial amount of cash."

"It makes financial sense seeing the back of me, I can tell," laughed Steph.

"Darling, we'll all be devastated. You're almost irreplaceable. But don't worry. I'll still write you a stunning reference. Now listen up, Bryony has news of her own as well."

Alana and Steph looked across the table expectantly.

Bryony grinned shyly and said, "Yes, I heard today I've just landed my first job. As a junior house officer at the Royal Free Hospital in Hampstead. It's only about three miles from where we live! I start there the moment I qualify, and I can pick up the surgery electives later!"

Alana topped up everyone's drink, and said "That's fantastic, Bry. Here's to new beginnings for all of us! Let's welcome 2020! Maybe it will be the best year ever!"

And Isabel and her friends all chinked their glasses together to the future.

Then Bryony said, "Oh, by the way, you know this virus they've had over in China...I think it might be more serious than we've been told. There are now cases reported in Northern Italy..."

THE END

I do hope you enjoyed reading this novel, the second in the series, "Isabel and friends".

If you did, please take a few minutes to leave a review on Amazon and/or Goodreads. Positive reviews make a huge difference to how many new readers try out a book, and are a huge encouragement to an author.

About the Author

This is Maggie McIntyre's fourth novel. She has writing for most of her life, and especially enjoys writing about women in love with women. She believes a good story can inspire, entertain and also console in times of trouble. It also has the power to break down barriers of hatred and fear between people, and help people live their lives to the full. Her home is in the north of England, but she travels extensively, especially these days to Spain and to the USA.

Find Maggie on her Facebook page, Maggie McIntyre Author and her website. www.maggiemcintyreauthor.com.

COMING SOON BY MAGGIE MCINTYRE

website: www.maggiemcintyreauthor.com
email: maggie@maggiemcintyreauthor.com

Into the Rough

Jane Walkley, out and proud, has been head of girls' P.E. at Redbridge High School for more than ten years. Her specialities as a coach are tennis and swimming, and she also plays a mean round of golf. She's fit, forty-two and her many friends assume she's happy being single. But Jane longs to find that special person, a woman she can commit to, a woman who will return her huge capacity for love, and so far, no-one has come anywhere close to her ideal.

When her best friend Isabel shocks her by marrying a young medical student and suddenly settling down, Jane feels even more abandoned. But then, Isabel introduces her to someone new, someone who presses all the right buttons, who intrigues and excites her.

There's just one problem, Isabel's friend Jenny is a renegade, disillusioned, but still committed nun, and Jane is a staunch atheist. Their fractious relationship can't possibly get past first post, or can it?

Set in England in 2020, the schools, gyms and leisure centres are all closed. What can Jane do to channel her energies, but try to convert stubborn Canadian Jenny to her way of thinking?

This is a love story for grown-up women deals with real-life choices, and is told with compassion and humour. It is the third book in the series, Isabel and Friends, and will be published in Spring 2021.

Other Great Books by Independent Authors

Isabel's Healing by Maggie McIntyre
A devastating car accident leaves Bel broken, but when a young assistant steps into her life, could Bel learn to live again?
Available from Amazon KDP (ISBN 9798650898733)

Heatwave by Maggie McIntyre
Will 'fresh out of school' Catriona Sinclair win over media mogul, Katherine Konrad, or will she get a little too close for comfort to the legend's notorious past?
Available from Amazon KDP (ISBN 9798677313929)

Wildfire by Maggie McIntyre
Sequel to Heatwave. An outing to meet Cat's family turns into a weekend fraught with danger. Will the challenges they face strengthen their love in the face of a natural disaster or will it prove too much to handle?
Available from Amazon KDP (ISBN 9798550424988)

Addie Mae by Addison M. Conley
At the beginning of a bitter divorce, Maddy meets mysterious Jessie Stevens. They bond over scuba diving, and as their friendship grows, so does the attraction.
Release scheduled for October 2020. (ISBN 9780998029641)

Call to Me by Helena Harte
Sometimes the call you least expect is the one you need the most.
Available from Amazon (ISBN 9781838066802)

Cosa Nostra by Emma Nichols
Will Maria choose loyalty to the Cosa Nostra or will she risk it all for love?
Available from Amazon (ISBN 9788636877899)

Other Great Books by Independent Authors

<u>Nights of Lily Ann: Redemption of Carly</u> by L L Shelton
Lily Ann makes women's desires come true as a lesbian escort, but can she help Carly, who is in search of a normal life after becoming blind.
Available from Amazon (ISBN 9798652694906)

<u>The Woman and The Storm</u> by Kitty McIntosh
Being the only witch in a small Scottish town is not easy.
Available from Amazon (ISBN 9798654945983)

<u>Sliding Doors</u> by Karen Klyne
Sometimes your best life is someone else's.
Available from Amazon (ISBN 9781916444386)

<u>Stealing a Thief's Heart</u> by C L Cattano
Two women, a great escape, and a quest for a soulmate.
Available from Amazon (ASIN B085DW2MZ7)

<u>Maddie Meets Kara: Remember Me</u> by D R Coghlan
Who is her enemy? Who is her friend? And what really happened that night?
Available from Amazon (ASIN B085WP5CDF)

<u>1140 Rue Royale</u> by Karen D. Badger
A gripping story of love and redemption in the most haunted mansion in New Orleans. (2017 GCLS Award Winner - Paranormal)
Available from Amazon and Badger Bliss Books (ISBN 9781945761003)

<u>Yesterday Once More</u> by Karen D. Badger
Will Jordan risk her own future to save the life of her lover who died before she was born? (2009 GCLS Award Winner – Speculative Fiction)
Available from Amazon and Badger Bliss Books (ISBN 9781945761027)

Other Great Books by Independent Authors

<u>Over The Crescent Moon</u> by Karen D. Badger
Spencer Bennet wakes up alone and injured on a deserted beach in Hawaii, only to find her world turned upside down.
(2019 LesFic Bard Award Winner in 2 categories – Action/Adventure & Historical)
Available from Amazon and Badger Bliss Books (ISBN 9781945761263)